CW01429346

WHEN THE SAX MAN PLAYS:

PART 1 MAKING IT

© YVONNE MARRS 2008/2013

Pauline,

I hope you enjoy
my first book!

Yvonne

WHEN THE SAX MAN PLAYS PART 1 MAKING IT

First edition published by Melrose Press in 2009.
Second edition published by WTSMP Publications in 2013.

A copy of this book is available from the British Library.

ISBN 978-0956994646

ACKNOWLEDGEMENTS

Thanks to my printing company, Imprint Digital, who have given me fantastic service for the printing of my books since day one!

As always, a big thanks to the guys at Sax London, who are always helpful, efficient and encouraging.

Last, but not least, my thanks to each and every member of the WTSMP fan club.

You know who you are!

WHEN THE SAX MAN PLAYS PART 1 MAKING IT
Chapter 1

Saxophone music carried on the breeze from the Music block. Such was the beauty of the piece that all conversation stopped; all earpieces were removed; all calls ended. The listeners looked around, concluding this was Impervious College's new Head of Music.

Jason reached the song's crescendo, oblivious to the attention he had captured. Taken aback by the rapturous applause, he blushed as several of his new female admirers wolf-whistled. He bowed in jest whilst unclipping the saxophone from around his neck to rest it once more in the protective case - until tonight's session: Jason held the 8 pm spot every Thursday at Fats Jazz Club.

Tucked away down a quiet alleyway, Fats was little-known to anyone except the Club's privileged regulars. It was the kind of place where everyone is family and no-one has any secrets; the perfect place for musicians to nurture their dreams. There was always someone on hand to give advice - whether it was required or not - no problem too big or small, always halved when shared. The supportive atmosphere was one that Jason would come to rely on in the near future, as yet he didn't know this would be the case.

Merciless taunting from his colleagues from that first week onwards ensued, as one of the senior tutors had drunkenly (and mistakenly, he assured the College elders) stumbled over the threshold one Thursday and witnessed, with his jaw dropped open, Jason playing the blues! Not much was remarked upon of his skill, just the young man/old scene jokery - which played rather like a stuck record, Jason thought to himself.

In the midst of one of these particular afternoon teases Jason's attention was brought to the Impervious Annual Talent Contest - and how Mr Seymour, Jason's predecessor, tutored a group to third place.

"From his own class, no doubt." Jason's lips formed the words and they were out before he could take them back.

"You wouldn't stand a chance otherwise!" Chambers (Mathematics and Applied Physics) declared, peering at him over his glasses.

Jason rose to the bait, to everyone's delight. "You'd have the same chance everyone else has!"

Thus Jason's challenge was issued: beat Seymour's third!

The following week found Jason quizzing his students, as a group and - as desperation struck - individually. The excuses varied: some true, some so pathetic he wondered... His gut reaction was that there was a conspiracy against him, but was it too soon to formulate that idea? He'd been in the job less than three weeks, surely such animosity did not belong in a College of such ranking as Impervious?

An anonymous note lay on his desk that afternoon: check the

College's blog. Jason remembered seeing the link some months previously when he was researching the College before attending his interview. No sooner had he found the Talent Contest thread, he came across the 'special message'.

"All Music students will be honoured with a bonus for concentrating on their studies, and not participating in the competition, which is beneath their collective talent."

His hand-picked group - gone!

Moments passed as he sat reeling from the blow, too stunned to see the fresh entry appear on the screen in front of him:

"No reason for the rest of the students to miss out on their shot at fame!"

Sitting in the solitude of the Music block, Jason was lost in his thoughts. His ultimate fear was one of failure: a fear only partially quashed by his talent. Music was the best thing in his life - it was his calling; it *was* his life.

To their dismay, he dismissed his parents' wish for him to study medicine, instead pursuing his music - and teaching. When he passed with merit, to his amazement Jason found he had his pick of jobs. His tutor had personally recommended him for this position at London's Impervious College and once he'd sailed through the interview, the position was his. His family continued to voice their thoughts that Music wasn't a proper subject. Unfortunately, the tutors at Impervious expressed the same thought, never letting up on the subject whenever he was within earshot.

Jason took a deep breath, summoning his courage. Despite the fact that it seemed the world was against him, he vowed with himself that he'd tutor a group for this ridiculous competition - he'd show them all!

The contest would be the making of him, in everyone's eyes, which explained why it was imperative that his group made the Final. Ultimately he wanted the title, of course, and that shouldn't be too difficult to achieve if none of the College's Music students were competing. Right?

Regularly now, there were many students listening to Jason's lunchtime playing. Today, Jason put the first stage of his plan into action, determined not to be thwarted before he'd begun. He pulled down the blind, displaying his poster to the outside world:

MUSIC ENTHUSIASTS REQUIRED TO WIN COMP!
MEETING AT 5 PM FRIDAY, MUSIC ROOM 1.

Pinning an identical notice on the student general notice board; the canteen notice board and the sports notice board, Jason considered all angles covered: if he failed, it wasn't for the lack of trying.

He swallowed hard. Failure, in any form, was not an idea he wanted to harbour. Would it shame him out of his job? The thought shook him to the core. Everything was built on his position at Impervious - his flat in central London; his growing self-esteem; his position at Fats. Without Impervious, he had nothing. The thought was sobering.

Jason sat in Music Room 1, musing that Friday had soon rolled around. Time had a strange sense of humour: his last class had finished half an hour ago - and yet five o'clock simply crawled around. He perched on the edge of his desk, eagerly waiting yet dreading a complete no-show!

Quarter past five came and the room remained empty. He began to mark some papers, wondering if there were any late lectures going on. Minutes later, he glanced at the wall clock: 5:28. How long, he wondered, feasibly could he stay?

"Auditions, here?" Kipper stuck his head round the door.

"Yes." Jason closed his folder, grinning at the young man in front of him. The grin threatened to split his face when he saw Dave behind Kipper. "Oh well, we'll have a trio anyway!" He joked, indicating for them to sit down.

"Sorry I'm late!" Vince rushed into the room, sinking into the nearest chair, some ten minutes later. "Couldn't get away." He murmured, aware suddenly that he was the centre of attention.

"Don't worry." Jason smiled at him. "You're here, that's the important thing!" He grinned at the three young men in front of him. "Let's introduce ourselves. As you may know, I'm Jason Bottelli, I'm 27 this year and I'm enjoying my role as Head of Music here. I graduated with top honours and I'm relishing the challenge of working at Impervious - and yes, I understand the name now!"

They all laughed.

"I've played sax since I was fourteen, and I can sing, though I prefer not to perform solo!"

More laughter filled the room.

"Ah! But I hear you do." Kipper challenged, crossing his arms in front of him. "Regularly at Fats Jazz Club."

Jason frowned. "How do you know that?"

"My brother's a regular with the Old Bros." Kipper smiled at him, seeing his awestruck expression.

Jason hoped the young man in front of him possessed some of that talent, hardly daring to ask. "Can you play?"

"I dabble, on the piano in the dining room."

Jason smiled. "There's nothing wrong with a dabble. Carry on, tell us about yourself."

"I'm Kipper Macleod, I'm 22 and I'm doing Media Studies and Acting. I'm lovin' the single life - the girls; the clubs; the parties..." He sighed happily.

From beside him, Dave rolled his eyes. "Yeah, that's you alright, the party animal!"

Jason laughed. "It takes all sorts to make a good team."

"Just as well," Dave muttered, much to Jason's amusement - and Kipper's annoyance.

"Tell us about yourself then." Jason locked eyes with Dave before their good-natured banter turned sour.

"He's the quiet one." Kipper interjected.

"That'll be to balance you out then?" Jason teased, seeing Dave smile appreciatively.

"I'm Dave, David Thompson, I'm 23 and in my final year of Business with French." He paused, usually people laughed when he announced his course. "But I can't play anything." He looked crestfallen.

"That's no problem Dave, I can teach you. I can teach anyone." He paused as Dave looked at him dubiously. "That's my job, remember?"

They all laughed, nodding.

Silence fell, and Vince caught Jason's eye. "I'm Vince Stewart, I'm also 23, and I'm doing English Lit. and Photography."

Jason was impressed. "That's quite a schedule, Vince."

Vince shrugged. "I'll cope - I'm a Stewart, we're famous for enduring hardship."

Kipper and Dave shared a look, which Jason caught. "It's up to you guys, it's your free time. I know you all have your studies."

"And jobs." Kipper added.

"Jobs?" Jason frowned, his mind filling with creeping doubts.

Vince nodded. "I'm a photographer's assistant at weekends."

"I work the clubs," Kipper began, seeing Jason frowning.

"He delivers the beer!" Dave explained, unable to contain his mirth.

"Yeah? We don't all have rich parents like you!" Kipper spat.

"You could've fooled me, Mr Piano-in-the-dining room!" Dave

rose to the challenge. "I work too, I run my commercial business from the spare room."

"Commercial?" Vince's eyes widened.

"Yeah - eBay!" Kipper roared with laughter.

Jason smiled, speaking louder. "So, can we all commit to this?" He received three nods, much to his growing relief.

"What's the timescale?" Vince asked.

"We have, initially, four weeks to choose a song and a name; decide on our positions... just the basics." Jason sighed. "The first stage begins in March, leading to the April final."

"That's not so bad." Kipper began consolingly. "We'll be fine, won't we?" He looked at Dave and Vince, getting them both to nod, before he turned back to Jason. "So, what's the deal? I heard they blackmailed the Music students."

Jason looked up. "Where did you hear that?"

"It's all over the Impervious blog, haven't you seen it?" Surprise sounded in Kipper's voice. "I thought, y'know, *you* would know all about it, you being young. The other lecturers are so old, they can't even suss out the 'signing in' page."

Everyone laughed.

"I'll look it up." Jason paused, changing the subject. "What type of music are you all into - jazz, classics, rock or a mixture?" He looked at each of them.

Kipper's answer didn't surprise him: "Rock."

"Something easy." Dave ventured.

"Yeah, me too, I'm quite open actually." Vince agreed.

Jason nodded. "That's good, but we need something that suits all of us." A shadow by the doorway caught his eye, causing him to turn around.

A shy young man hovered there, reddening with the attention the four turned on him. "I'm really sorry I couldn't get here any quicker."

"Don't worry." Jason gave him a warm smile. "Come in and join us - this is Kipper, Dave and Vince, and I'm Jason."

"I know who you are." The newest member of the band smiled back, taking his seat quickly, folding his hands in his lap, his shoulder bag still slung over his thin body.

Jason hid his frown, unsure of what to make of the new recruit, trying not to rely on first impressions.

"I've heard you play, you're excellent." He continued quietly, his gaze landing in his lap.

Jason saw Kipper and Dave exchange another look.

"Thanks." Jason beamed at him when his gaze was met. "Tell us about yourself - Kipper's an aspiring actor, Dave's an entrepreneur, and Vince is the photographer."

"I'm Michael Johns, I'm only 18. I didn't get on in school. I'm doing Drama." He paused. "I can't play, but I can sing."

Kipper tried to hide his snort, but failed miserably.

Jason shot him a look that silenced him. "That's great. We were discussing what music we like, we're generally a mixture with me of course having the jazz background. What's your favourite?"

"I don't have one." He smiled at Jason again, his eyes barely flitting over the rest of the group. "I'm easy."

Kipper groaned and hid his head in his hands.

Dave thumped him. "Ignore him," he said before anyone else spoke. "He's a jerk most of the time, but he's alright really. Would you shut up and let Mike finish?" He said, thumping Kipper again.

"Watch it!" Kipper brushed him off.

Dave rolled his eyes but they were both smiling.

Mentally taking a step back from the room, Jason was struck with the notion that he had quite a handful of characters here.

"Will you be a part of the band?" Michael asked the question everyone else was dying to ask, all four looking at Jason, which brought him back to the present.

Jason nodded. "If it's deemed necessary, yes I will."

"We'd be raw without your experience." Vince observed.

"We'll see." Jason hid his laughter, glad that *someone* thought highly of him, recalling his family's dismay and that of his fellow lecturers, before returning to the current situation. "I'll compile several songs I think we could perform - can you four also do that?" He received four nods. "We need a name too - and to sort instruments and positions." Another four nods. "Perhaps Kipper, keyboard would suit you - as you say you 'dabble' on the piano."

Kipper's face lit up, and he followed Jason to the back of the room, taking the set of headphones from him and sitting in the adjacent chair as directed. Jason opened a music book in front of him and played the first line, which was repeated in the second, third and fourth. Kipper picked up on this and played it exactly. Jason showed him the next page, explaining the arrangements increased in difficulty, leaving him to practice in peace with the headphones plugged in, feeling secretly relieved that at least one of his recruits was musically minded.

He turned to Dave, Vince and Michael. The quiet one; the survivor and - the thought flashed through his mind before he could stop it - the *gay* youngster; not that this posed a problem. Unless his admiration for Jason was more than friendly. He swallowed hard, silently pleading that this was not going to be the case, not sure how he would cope in such a situation...

"We'll need a drummer, keyboard player," he paused, indicating Kipper, "and guitarist, plus vocals. Don't worry if we don't conclude positions tonight, there's plenty time." He smiled at the nervous-looking three in front of him. "We'll start with the drums, see if any of you have a natural aptitude. You never know." He added, seeing the dubious look Dave was giving him. Already he had formed an idea of each young man in his mind. Dave was the one with the low self-esteem, but Jason was sure that with the right coaching, he could crack his confidence problem. He seemed a strong character - to be able to rebound off Kipper and shrug off his otherwise hurtful comments he had to be - which showed some promise.

Kipper was the one with the egotistical, perfectionist nature. He wasn't the most handsome of the band, as far as Jason would admit, but he could see girls following the band because of him. He oozed charisma, which wasn't necessarily a bad quality in a band member.

Vince seemed the quiet type. Quiet, but social when the occasion demanded it - his choice of courses told that story for him. What puzzled Jason was why Vince was interested in the band - he already had a heavy workload, on top of his weekend work. He had been surprised when Vince had shown early empathy for him, wondering if he would always side with him on their group disagreements? He hoped at least to have one person on his side: it would be nice to have an ally!

And then there was Michael: well-mannered and well-meaning, and he had plenty enthusiasm. Being young he may be naive, but he would perhaps be more receptive to the group's ideas.

Jason surmised that Michael and Vince would be the easiest to work with. Dave's lack of confidence would create obstacles, as would Kipper's stubborn streak. He knew he would need a staunch supporter: pegging Vince as favourite to fill this position.

After twenty minutes of practice at drums and guitar, Michael requested a quiet word with Jason, who'd winced through the whole ear-torturing exercise. "I'd like to just stick to vocals." Jason raised his eyebrows in interest.

"I've got a bit of a talent," he said shyly. "My dad's a big jazz fan, we always sing along to the old records."

Here goes, Jason thought to himself, *he thinks he's a crooner!*

"Really?" Trying to keep his voice neutral, he continued. "I have

no records but I could play; would you be able to sing along,
unaccompanied? It's very different to having backing vocals."

"Why not?" Michael smiled, admiration reflected in his gaze.
Jason felt his heart pound. There was no way he was putting
himself in a room alone with Michael: the implications for his
career were too much.

He looked at Dave and Vince, who took an immediate break,
having overheard the conversation.

In three long strides, Jason had unplugged Kipper and whipped
the songbook from beside him, passing it to Michael. "Find a
song that you feel familiar with, and we'll start there."
Michael swallowed hard, his hands shaking. "Here?"
Jason nodded. "You have to get used to an audience, at least
you're starting with a friendly one."
Silence fell as Michael scrutinised the songs, page by page.
Jason cast his eye over the rest of the band, seeing they were
equally intrigued by this strange youngster. Suddenly Michael
was beaming at him, the book open on "Englishman in New
York".
Jason too smiled. "Ah, yes. Good rhythm, catchy and a little
challenging - the perfect song for us." He undid the clasps on the
saxophone case, slipping the sling around his neck and clipping
the instrument to his chest.

He loved the feel of the instrument; he knew all the curves of
his oldest and best friend blindfold. Just holding the instrument
soothed him at the highest, indescribable level. Already man and

instrument had survived much private turmoil, and Jason knew the journey was far from over.

"Kipper, count us in please, to three." He nodded at Michael, who nodded his readiness. There was no time to think in those three seconds: Jason immediately slipped into playing mode, his mind blank, allowing the music to flow through his body. The band members were spellbound by Michael's voice, bursting into applause when they finished.

"He made the song sound like it was written for him!" Dave whistled, shaking his head. "You're brilliant. Where did you learn to sing like that, Mike?"

Michael was blushing beetroot from his band mates' attention and praise. He shrugged.

"It doesn't matter." Kipper grinned at Michael, banging him heartily on the back. "This calls for a celebration, let's go to the Union Bar!"

Jason stood watching as they left, with Michael swept up in their wake. Hastily, he re-cased his trusty saxophone, following them. It was quite obvious that their first meeting had been a success, and a drink was a good celebration. This was nothing short of a miracle: two talented band members, and two with promise. 'Miracle'! Jason's smile widened: the band's name was born.

Chapter 2

Jason smiled smugly to himself as his fellow lecturers tried to wind him up the following Monday morning. He stirred his coffee in silence, waiting for them to fall into their own trap.

"Bottelli, Fred tells me no-one arrived for your meeting." Avery (Art and Graphic Design) smiled.

Jason paused for effect. "I'm afraid you have misunderstood. Actually, I had four successful auditions - and we arranged our positions and concocted a band name, all in one sitting. Not bad for a night's work." He grinned.

This was met with a frown, and some confusion.

"You were seen heading to the Union Bar alone, Bottelli." Chambers (Maths and Applied Physics) shook his head.

Jason's smile widened. "The auditions finished rather quickly and in celebration, I will admit. You can ask Smithy; we each paid a round."

Douglas (Chemistry) roared. "Drinking with students is no way for any lecturer of this College to behave!"

Resting his mug on the sideboard, Jason folded his arms across his chest. "How I spend my free time is nobody else's business." Several lecturers fumed at Jason's defiance.

"I have done nothing wrong. Good morning, gentlemen." Jason turned on his heel, collecting his half-empty mug on his way out.

Jason felt good about himself. He truly had done nothing wrong; and anyway, it had been a social occasion where the

band could bond. There was nothing illicit about that at all.
Indeed Jason foresaw many such meetings at the Union Bar, it
was the best place for the students to be themselves.

They had decided that he was definitely playing - Jason was as
much a part of Miracle as the rest of them - as he was the one
who would secure them victory. Admittedly Vince and Kipper
were plastered when they announced this, but they all knew the
truth in those words. Dave, Michael and Jason weren't drinkers;
so Kipper was pleased to find a new drinking partner in Vince.

Alcohol or no alcohol, they all relaxed in the Union Bar, giving
Jason a chance to learn why each young man had auditioned.

Kipper saw it as a chance to get his foot in the door of the
acting world; "another feather in his cap" were his exact words.
Jason nodded to himself, knowing this made sense and feeling
glad that Kipper was so egotistical - as if this one small success
would have such a spectacular result! There was, however, no
harm in letting him work under such pretence.

Dave hoped to build his self-confidence, making them pledge
to do their utmost to help him achieve this. Jason nodded again,
seeing a part of himself in the youngster.

Vince was in it to get the woman of his dreams as he had a
string of failed relationships and wanted a woman to excite, thrill
and inspire him! Secretly Jason wondered if he too suffered from
low self-esteem, knowing that time would tell.

Michael too was after the fame. His participation allowed him
to fulfil a childhood fantasy.

WHEN THE SAX MAN PLAYS PART 1 MAKING IT

Jason swallowed hard hearing the word 'fantasy', changing the subject; sharing with them his hope that Miracle would reach the Final. He knew this was the band's shared dream, and as one, they vowed to give their all to achieve this ambition.

Jason mulled over these thoughts as his coffee steamed. He'd remained in the Music block for his afternoon break, plugging in the tiny kettle at the back of Music Room 1 - the least used of the rooms in the section - leaning back in the comfy chair.

His laptop sat on the clutter-free work surface as he played the compilation that he'd concocted over the weekend. The songs were a mix of genres: some suited the group as a whole; some were his favourites; some were specifically suited for Michael's voice; others had fabulous pieces from the electric guitar with the perfect backing of, yes, drums and keyboard.

He reviewed the band members' reasonings, knowing it was only human to want to succeed; to fit in; to have fun and enjoy life. These were emotions he'd stumbled across throughout his teenage years, having lived in his older brother's shadow for his entire life. His demanding, and at times unreasonable, parents only added to this pain. How on Earth they thought he would succeed in the medical world...!

Jason shook his head with his thoughts. Was there job satisfaction in such a responsible profession? There were so many places for error to creep into your work - and affect someone's life long-term, for good or bad.

WHEN THE SAX MAN PLAYS PART 1 MAKING IT

Jason knew there was an element of responsibility in his job - he had to teach the students, whether they wanted to learn or not - but he was relieved that he could leave it all behind at the end of the day; close the door and walk away. It wasn't so easy for Christopher.

Jason shook his head, thinking about his brother: his rock through the hard times; his only supporter. He pondered his next thought, savouring the excitement that filled him - Christopher may get behind this challenge. His parents certainly wouldn't, they had nothing to do with him since he left for University years ago: cards and letters went unanswered. Being a diligent son he continued to make contact; in the hope that one day they would celebrate his achievements together. Deep down, a voice told him this day would never come. It was a difficult notion to get his head around: however, he believed their attitude had toughened him against the hardness of an unforgiving world.

"That sounds great, who is it?" Michael's voice cut through his thoughts, making Jason jump, spilling his coffee over the desk. They both mopped at the liquid; one apologising, one forgiving.

"I'm not disturbing you, am I?" He continued.

"No, I'm just mulling over a few ideas." Jason smiled at him, consulting his watch and seeing his next class was due soon.

His schedule was one that he cursed: one that seemed half full, not one weekday completely taken with lessons, which he found more than a little strange. This made him delve deeper into Impervious' history - and he'd been surprised what he'd found.

"I came to drop this off, between classes." Michael pulled a CD out of his bag, returning his smile. "Thank you for taking me on."

Jason smiled at him. "How could I refuse a voice like that?"

Michael's gaze dropped. "I'm a burden, not being able to play."

Jason waved his hand casually in Michael's direction, as if to wave away his words, and his fear. "That doesn't matter, especially as you were all so insistent on having me play."

Michael's face turned into one big grin. "You're so good, we're bound to make the Final!"

Jason laughed. "I like your optimism!"

Michael nodded eagerly, leaving after a quick goodbye. Jason watched the space he'd filled only seconds ago, shaking his head in wonder. He would have to tread very carefully from now on. God forbid if Michael got any ideas about their working partnership developing!

The days soon flew by, until it was Thursday. Thursdays were always special to Jason as they marked his performance at Fats.

The Club's owner, Glenn, had made a few suggestions to him recently regarding his performances, and as Kipper had reported to the group, he did a little singing with his set - soon he planned to link up with two other jazz musicians, also Fats regulars. The trio would be well received, he felt sure.

All in all, it was a perfect set-up, Jason knew he was incredibly lucky to have fallen on his feet in this way. He ran his theories for the Impervious competition by his friends at Fats, who backed him earnestly, building on his own ideas.

Friday evening soon rolled around, bringing nerves twisting in his stomach. What if the band decided they weren't interested after all? The thought filled him with dread.

He knew he could count on Michael's support. Looking back, he could only see signs of positivity from the rest of the group, however... Relief washed over him when they arrived together half an hour later.

He laughed aloud. "I was wondering if you lot had changed your minds!"

Laughter echoed around the room as Jason was handed three CDs, and everyone looked at Michael.

"I already gave mine in." He paused, his face reddening from their collective attention. "I figured Jason would be swamped with four in one go." His gaze dropped shyly to his feet.

"You were right. We might've be here all night otherwise!" Jason joked. "Let's play the first one." He fed the first disc into his laptop and clicked 'play'.

"What the hell is *this*?!" Kipper hid his head in his hands, as if to block out the music.

Jason fought his urge to laugh.

"This is a classic. I might've known you wouldn't recognise it, with your *cultured* background." Dave rolled his eyes. "Skip to the next one, it's more modern." He instructed Jason, seeing nobody was enjoying the piece.

WHEN THE SAX MAN PLAYS PART 1 MAKING IT

"You're so old!" Kipper groaned, barely letting the first bar of the song finish, shaking his head.

However, Dave was pleased to see that he - and the others - were looking a little more interested.

Silence fell as the track finished.

"Put mine on next, the silver and blue case." Kipper demanded. Jason's eyebrows raised in interest, wondering what they were in for. Amongst the tracks Kipper had selected, one stood out: it was a Sting version of "Englishman in New York" with several fabulous saxophone passages.

Vince's creation was next and Jason wondered what the disc would hold. Kipper's had the rock vibe; Dave's was so classical it was almost mesmerising; Michael's CD had been a mixture of old and new music. One of Vince's songs was almost perfect but had female vocals - Kipper ripped him to shreds over the issue.

"But that can be worked around." Vince said, in his own defence. "It's the bare bones of the song that are important." Michael cleared his throat. "You're forgetting who your lead vocalist is, aren't you?"

"You couldn't pitch that high." Kipper stated, eyeballing him, daring him to argue.

Michael took the bait. "I'm sure I could with the right training."

"Private tuition." Jason mused. "A lot of hard work, and months we simply don't have." He shrugged. "I like it personally, and I agree it could work. But first, I want to play you something." He tapped a few keys and music rolled from the speakers.

Kipper moaned. "George Michael?! Are you for real?!"

Jason was grinning at them. "Damn right I am." He laughed as Michael automatically joined in with the chorus.

"No way!" Kipper scraped his chair back noisily, getting to his feet in protest. "I'm not playing a gay song!"

Jason challenged him. "It's only a gay song if that's your first memory of it."

"What does that mean?!" Kipper was at Jason's chair in two long strides, his expression thunderstruck.

"It means what I said." Jason stood up, looking him in the eye, showing that he would not be threatened. "It fits perfectly - there's great opportunity for drums, guitar and piano."

Kipper hesitated in mid-argument. "Piano?"

"You said you'd played, right?" Jason watched as Kipper nodded, continuing before he could start talking again. "As you're all so adamant that I play, the song has to fit with saxophone - that's no easy task, if you haven't already noticed." He paused, watching the expressions on Kipper's face change to confused, and then interested. "So," he took a deep breath, "is the direction we're going to take?"

"I'm in." Vince said, almost instantly. "It's popular, it'll engage the crowd and it'll win - if we get it right."

"It's virtually written for me." Michael grinned at Jason and Vince. "Count me in."

Jason smiled, and the three turned to look at Dave and Kipper.

Dave was looking nervously at his friend before looking again at Jason. "You're sure there's nothing else that would suit us?"

Jason shrugged. "You're welcome to research it."

"We will." Kipper and Dave spoke together.

"Bear in mind we need to have it rehearsed in three weeks so that we can place our entry." Jason reminded them.

"Three weeks?" Kipper repeated, astonished.

Jason nodded solemnly.

"But you agree to hear it, whatever we find?"

"Of course." Jason gave him a beaming smile of encouragement and looked at Vince and Michael. "We'll give it a fair hearing, won't we guys?"

The pair nodded.

"I can go higher, but not deeper." Michael pointed out.

"Nothing too rock." Vince added. "We don't want to put the judges off or we'll never make the Semis, never mind the Final."

Jason's grin widened, so clear was his relief that everyone was thinking positively - and in the last stages of the contest! What a dream that would be, and how it would wipe the self-centred smiles from the faces of his colleagues.

"We accept the challenge." Kipper said, crossing his arms over his chest in typical battle body language.

"If you can't match us, you'll work with us on our choice?" Jason asked, taking in the conflicting emotions on Kipper's face.

Two nods were all the confirmation that they needed. The band broke up for the weekend, agreeing to meet the following Friday where any other ideas would be put forward and the final vote would be cast.

Kipper was determined to get his own way, and his own song; unaware that Vince had harboured the same burning ambition - only he'd embraced "Careless Whisper" because it was the perfect song for them. Jason was right, all their instruments fell into place and the song itself was relatively easy to play. Vince knew when he was beaten, wondering if he'd ever get a chance to take charge...

Chapter 3

Georgie Jones had been a studious academic her whole life. By three years old, she could read and write; her Summers were spent at 'camp' learning new skills. Her life was mapped out for her by the time she started school at four-and-a-half: she would follow family tradition to become a lawyer.

Her parents were both successful barristers for London firms and thought this was a wise career for their only daughter. Fortunately, Georgie took to Law like a duck to water. She was in her final few months at Impervious and set to sail through her exams, expecting to graduate with top honours.

She was looking forward to graduating and had agreed to go on holiday with her three girlfriends, Leanne, Sophie and Anna, when they were all finished.

The realisation was dawning slowly upon Georgie that she'd never lived! (Leanne's words one night after they'd consumed a few bottles of wine.) Her drinking and socialising was minimalist. She'd never gambled - not even bingo? Sophie had asked - nor lied about her age; nor sneaked uninvited in to a party or had drunken sex.

Anna changed the subject. "How about truth or dare?"

Georgie's face wrinkled in disgust.

"C'mon, it'll be fun!" Anna hiccupped, nudging her. "Soph, you start."

"Okay, Lee?" Sophie turned to Leanne.

"Truth." Leanne smiled, a little the worse for drink.

"How many men have you slept with - and who was your best, and worst?"

"That's three truths!" Leanne half laughed, half protested.

"Answer the question." Anna too laughed with her friends.

"Fifteen," Leanne paused. "Worst? Ryan - he built me up and then couldn't get it up: he was too drunk! Best was Nick - he's a dream." She sighed happily, much to the amusement of her friends. "My turn, Anna - truth or dare?"

"Dare." Amusement danced in Anna's eyes.

Leanne went to the bar and returned with a shot glass, placing it in front of her. "I dare you to down this in one."

"What is it?" Georgie asked the question on everyone's lips.

"Ahh," Leanne tapped the side of her nose, knowingly. Well, it would've been knowingly, if she hadn't been too drunk to actually touch her nose.

"Easy!" Anna grabbed the tiny glass, raising it to her lips and pouring the contents down her throat. Her face immediately reddened. She spluttered and coughed, downing Georgie's lemonade in an attempt to extinguish the flames engulfing her throat. "Water!" She croaked, fanning her face.

The girls laughed.

Leanne then gave her the pint of iced water the barman offered her earlier, explaining. "Chilli-mix. 'A 19% concoction of pure fire'." She quoted from the bottle.

"It's burnt a layer of skin off my throat!" Anna managed, her voice still croaky from the shock.

Her friends all laughed, despite their concern.

"My turn?" Georgie asked her. "I choose truth. Think carefully."

Anna considered this. "Which one of the lecturers do you fancy the most?"

Georgie's face reddened. Her expression was priceless.

"Don't play innocent." Sophie warned, laughing into her drink.

"You like him, that Music man, don't you? New lecturer... James, no; Jim, no. What's his name?" Leanne trailed off.

"Jason." Georgie said quietly.

"That's him!" Leanne grinned at her. "Don't blame you girl, he's a real dish!"

Georgie smiled. "Have you heard him play? What a talent!"

"Play?" Leanne repeated, dismayed to find her glass was empty - for the fifth time that night. Each glass seemed to empty quicker than the last!

"We hang around by the Music block at lunch and listen. He plays the saxophone. You said it was beautiful." Georgie reminded her.

"Did I?" Leanne's voice began to slur. "Don't 'member."

"You did." Anna agreed. "You said how handsome he is, and how a man's feet equal the size of his..."

Leanne grinned at her friends. "I 'member now!"

Georgie and Anna rolled their eyes, while Sophie laughed. "Is that how you size up a man? That's where I'm going wrong - I'm looking them in the face and you're looking at his shoes."

Her laughter was infectious; soon they were all laughing
hysterically. Relieved the moment had passed, Georgie was
unaware the conversation would haunt her for a lot longer than a
night.

"Where did we get to last night?" Leanne yawned, gripping her
folder that was threatening to slip to the floor. Her other hand
was holding the yellow handle swinging from the roof of the
Tube carriage. She stood for their journey, convinced that if she
sat down she'd fall asleep and they'd leave her travelling around
the Circle line all morning until she woke.

"Nancy's, don't you remember?" Sophie teased, hiding a yawn
of her own. It seemed as if her seven o'clock alarm had gone off
too early... mind you, it always did in her opinion.

Leanne rolled her eyes, yawning again. "With our Georgie." Her
hazel eyes settled on Georgie's tired complexion. "How far did
we get with the plan?"

"What plan?" Georgie's eyes widened.

"The plan to get you and Jason together."

"Sshh! People can hear you!" Georgie was mortified. She
couldn't believe they were having this conversation on the Tube
- *the* most public place, ever.

"Forget them." Leanne let go of the handle to wave Georgie's
fear away, almost landing in Georgie's lap as the train braked.
"He's nice. You got me thinking, it's perfect you'll soon be
leaving, so it won't mean any trouble."

WHEN THE SAX MAN PLAYS PART 1 MAKING IT

"But... but..." Georgie stammered.

Anna squeezed Georgie's knee fondly. "You need a man."

"I'm looking forward to having time to myself." Georgie sighed.

Sophie smiled at her from across the carriage. "Anna's right, a steady relationship would do you good. Jason's just the type to be a woman's rock."

Georgie roared with laughter, now oblivious to the listeners around them. "How would you know that?" She paused, a thought striking her. "Oh God, Soph! You haven't!"

Sophie's pretty pale face creased into a frown. "No! I'd love to, but no." She shook her head. "I just know men like him. You're the one who said you wanted commitment. The older guys are more ready." Sophie stopped in mid-thought. She sighed, swallowing the lump in her throat, thinking about her ex, Simon. He'd wanted everything - marriage, house, kids, but she felt trapped; rushed and frightened...

"It wouldn't do any harm to get to know him." Georgie began.

"Indeed!" Anna grinned at her, looping her arm through Georgie's as the train drew into their station and the four alighted. "We'll plan for you to start as friends and if it's meant to be, it'll happen."

Leanne scoffed. "Yeah, right."

"It's true. What is meant to be, will be." Anna continued.

"I agree - I'm meant to do Law, and I've landed a fab job, even before I've finished my Degree." Georgie beamed.

"There must be some truth in that." Sophie nodded.

WHEN THE SAX MAN PLAYS PART 1 MAKING IT

Leanne rolled her eyes. "Anyway! I've an idea."

"It's too early to deal with your ideas, Lee." Anna groaned.

Sophie laughed. "I think we need a coffee before you tell us."
They turned left out of the station, walking the route they took every day to Impervious, stopping off at their favourite coffee house. Once inside, they devoured the delicious smells. The pristine white counter top always shone, whether or not the sun was out. Beyond the counter, the stainless steel drinks machines gleamed, competing for customers' attention. The man behind the counter looked up as they approached.

"Ah! My favourite customers! How are you this morning, ladies? You look tired - was it a late studying night?" He laughed, automatically preparing their regular order - three coffees and a hot chocolate for Georgie, who refrained from the caffeine boost her friends relied on to get them through the day.

"There'll be a lot of coffee at MacMillan's." Leanne always teased her. "You'll have to get used to it, sooner or later."
Georgie shook her head, exchanging her cup for a note, thanking him, careful to leave a decent tip. Her thoughts came full-circle: Jason Bottelli, the new Music tutor. His name sounded Italian, and Georgie was immediately drawn to her memories of her favourite holiday: the villa in the Italian lakes. Her face broke into a broad smile.

"She's thinking about him again." Leanne nudged Sophie seeing Georgie smile.

All four of them laughed as they made their way to Impervious.

Chapter 4

Kipper was still annoyed on Monday morning: in fact, his misdirected anger helped secure him the lead gangster role in this week's class performance. He was annoyed about the lack of music he'd come across that fitted Miracle. He had spent the weekend, once he had finished the pub deliveries, scouring his music collection, and then *hours* online. Nothing fitted.

Well, the songs that did were either total crap (in his opinion) or too high for Michael's voice. He knew that Jason would only entertain a song that suited every band member, and this was the hardest part. Admitting defeat late on Sunday evening, he decided to call Dave, knowing his mate would have the same result to report.

"Actually." Dave grinned smugly, pausing for effect. "I have."

"What?" Kipper spluttered, nearly choking on his mouthful of lukewarm beer. He pulled a face; he'd been so engrossed in his search, he'd opened it some three hours previously and promptly forgot.

Still! Kipper was annoyed that *he* hadn't come up with it. The song was a definite contender: it was "Englishman in New York" - the song Michael had sung at their original audition.

Kipper mused over setting up their own band if Jason didn't give them a fair hearing. How hard would it be? You entered, you practised, you won. Only the best on the night would win, and there was only one winner - and he was damn sure he would be a part of that winning group!

He worked furiously on the piano piece for "Englishman in New York", having immediately disconnected from Dave's call and downloaded the song composition in the small hours of Monday morning. Dave's drumming would come along, after all, how hard was it to tap out the same rhythm over and over? With a bit of cajoling, Kipper was sure Jason would play with them... after all, Jason *ached* to win. Happiness crept over him: the plan was foolproof!

As the class reflected upon the author's words; the thinking behind the chosen turn of phrase that he used throughout the novel, Vince found himself drifting.

Everything happened for a reason; Fate always showed a guiding hand when he was struggling. The band was his key to a better existence, he felt sure. His involvement would progress his non-starter relationships with the ladies, and he hoped that it would also lead him to the love of his life.

Was it that hard? People fell in love all the time. Sure, he wasn't the most handsome of the band members; he wasn't the one in the spotlight as Michael would be. But still, he was in the band. The winning band, they collectively hoped!

Vince looked at his list: some list - there were two artists! Jason's song *was* by far and away the best. He wondered if Dave and Kipper had drawn the same conclusion. Their next band meeting would be interesting---

WHEN THE SAX MAN PLAYS PART 1 MAKING IT

Jason too was in a reflective mood that Monday morning. He was in love with his new life - he was striding out on his own: his job, his qualification, his own place and soon his own band. His only relationship was with music; the band was such a Godsend, it was the ultimate distraction.

Christopher had slid the word 'girlfriend' into last week's usual monthly meeting and Jason froze mid-conversation.

"You said your life is going so well." Christopher had remarked. "So this is the best time. You have no responsibilities - you can have fun." He had sighed then. "Neither do you work long, tiresome hours."

Jason had made Christopher laugh telling him about Miracle, and how much hard work he foresaw getting the band up to scratch; silently nodding when he was told that it wouldn't just be his hard work. Jason just hoped that everyone gave the 110% they'd promised.

He was pleased to witness the progress of some of his most gifted music students: the ones who wanted to be there and really make something of themselves. Already Jason was making headway forcing out the few lacklustre students: late arrivals, broken instruments and devil-may-care attitudes. His quiet hour on Friday was scheduled for a meeting with the College's Principal, Hamish, where the "expellation letters" would be signed and sent to said pupils, making classes more relaxed (for Jason) and more productive (for the rest). Already time was in a hurry this semester - the first six weeks had simply flown by.

WHEN THE SAX MAN PLAYS PART 1 MAKING IT

Hamish Maclean's office was a shrine to his Scottish origins: bedecked in Maclean tartan (though everyone secretly doubted the authenticity of the tartan's name) and corresponding crimson walls. He always greeted Jason like a long-lost friend, something that never failed to cheer him - and something he noticed not every lecturer received. There could, of course, be many reasons for this, yet Jason's subconscious couldn't think of any.

They chatted conversationally, politely, as Hamish signed Jason's small pile of letters. Looking up at him once the letters were signed and sealed, Hamish asked how preparations with Miracle were coming along? Jason's look of astonishment made Hamish roar with laughter.

"I know everything, my boy." Hamish tapped the side of his nose conspiratorially. "Don't hold back." He gave Jason his warmest smile. "They're a rotten lot, the Impervious lecturers. They always think they outclass the new tutors, because they've been here since the Year Dot." He rubbed his hands together with glee. "I can't wait to see their faces when you succeed." Suddenly Jason was consumed with disgust: his face darkened.

"There will be no fixing, don't look at me like that!" Hamish was appalled at Jason's unspoken thought. "You will succeed only *because of your talent*. I heard the boy sing, what's his name?"

"Michael." Jason's voice was barely a squeak.

"Your tenor sax is, naturally, superb. The drummer," Hamish hesitated and Jason realised he was waiting for the correct name.

"Vince."

"Vince will hold it together with practice. As will your guitarist - bass or electric?"

"Bass I think, but I'm open to ideas." Jason said quickly.

"David Thompson, if I'm not mistaken. Nice lad, Dave. Not sure about that fellow with him - Kipper?" Hamish frowned. Jason nodded. "A little egotistical, but a talent on the ivories. Bucketful of charisma; knows how to charm a crowd."

Hamish wasn't convinced. "He's trouble that one."

"Needs a firm hand of guidance, that's all." Jason said, trying to believe his own words.

"Needs more than that I'd say, but it's your call." Hamish shrugged. "Good luck."

"Thank you." Jason smiled, shaking Hamish's hand, sweeping up the letters before he left, hardly daring to draw breath before he was out of the office and heading towards the Music block.

He left the letters on his desk, sinking into his chair, toying with the idea of having the Principal's vote. A silent thrill rippled through him, playing a triumphant smile on his lips.

Leanne nudged Georgie, snapping her from her thoughts.

"Sorry," Georgie frowned. "What did I miss?"

"Where were you - a million miles away?" Sophie teased her.

Anna sighed. "Yeah, desert island; hammock; G&T on tap; hunky man with huge..."

"Stop!" Georgie laughed.

"...palm leaf, I was going to say!" Anna laughed. "I don't know what you were thinking, Georgie." She said innocently, all four descending into laughter.

Leanne repeated herself. "What do you think to the plan?"

"It's great." Georgie beamed at her. "But there are three flaws. One - I'm not exactly gorgeous band-material. Two - I can't sing or play anything, I can't even dance! And three - the band is complete, they don't need me."

Leanne snorted. "They need you - they need sex appeal."

"They have sex appeal." Anna said quietly, thinking about Kipper. "I know he's an air-head but he has *it*."

"No." Sophie shook her head determinedly. "I know what you mean Lee. They need female sex appeal - Impervious isn't all women. Thank God!"

"Impervious has 47% of a male population." Leanne quoted.

"What?!" Georgie spluttered. "Where are these men hiding?"

"And the judging panel is all male." Sophie continued, sharing a knowing look with Leanne.

Georgie cringed. Her friends were in league to get her into this, there was no chance of escape. But there was nothing they could do about the three flaws - could they?

"As for your three flaws," Sophie paused for effect, "one - we can fix you up, there's a stunning girl under there." She waved her hand over Georgie's solemn attire. "Two - we can teach you to sing and dance."

Georgie pounced. "Ah! However, flaw three still exists."

Leanne shrugged. "Bands will come and go."

It was Anna's turn to pounce. "What do you know?"

Leanne's gaze dropped. "It's only a rumour."

"Oh?" Sophie paused, interested. "Since when did that ever stop you? Spill!"

"If you're trying to make trouble, you can take it elsewhere!" Jason roared. "There's enough to do without you dragging your heels!"

"I want that fair hearing you promised." Kipper crossed his arms in front of him, standing his ground.

"You'll get a fair hearing, as long as I get your commitment no matter what the outcome." Jason's tone turned to quiet malice.

"Sure." Kipper cleared his throat. "We came up with this."

With a flourish he produced the CD, playing it to the group. Jason broke the silence that had fallen after the song finished.

"Very original." He rolled his eyes. "But it's not *catchy* enough."

"What the hell's catchy got to do with it?" Kipper spat.

"It's gotta be catchy to get the votes." Dave said quietly, in fear of his friend's response.

Kipper spun round, glaring at him. "So you're with him now?"

"I'm just telling you the truth." He shrugged. "It's not my fault if you don't like it."

Kipper visibly fumed.

Silently, Jason was counting to ten. "I suggest you come back when you've had a chance to calm down and collect your thoughts." He spoke when Kipper's eyes found his.

WHEN THE SAX MAN PLAYS PART 1 MAKING IT

"Are you kicking me out?" Anger flashed in Kipper's eyes. "I
don't need you - I can win without you!"

"That would be interesting." Jason turned away from him,
walking round his desk to sit down.

All eyes fell on Kipper, all tension in the room defused.

Jason smiled when the door slammed behind Kipper, seeing the
rest of the band wince. "Don't worry about him. Once he learns
to get over himself, he'll be fine."

The group dissolved into relieved laughter.

The more Georgie pondered the idea, the more she liked it. She
wasn't sure about the details though - how would she work with
Jason if she was with the band that split from the main group?

Impervious was rife with the rumour that Jason's hand-picked
squad were disbanding already, even before the entries were
initially submitted!

To become pawn in the middle of this game sounded like a
very bad idea. However, Georgie relished a challenge, and she
liked the idea of spending time with Jason - albeit in the
tutor/student role - but she was due to graduate soon, so that
wouldn't be a problem. She had laughed her way through the
Saturday night dance classes with the girls; they were great fun
and good for improving her fitness.

Still, that didn't solve the fact that she couldn't sing. Her dull
voice was too low to hit the high notes that professional female
vocalists achieved. She confessed her fears to her friends and

was amazed a few days later when Anna put headphones over her ears and slipped the tiny music player into her hand.

"Your wish is granted." She smiled at Georgie.

Kipper was quiet at the following week's practice session, but he worked hard. Jason had to admire him from that aspect: he was determined to succeed, though he still made it obvious he hated the song of their choice. Jason shrugged his complaints off, and eventually Kipper realised his grievance was falling on deaf ears - even he knew when to call a halt.

Jason entered Miracle with "Careless Whisper", his heart beating faster when he was told they'd be in the first night of auditions as they were one of the first entries.

There was a notice up by the end of the week confirming all entries and auditions. Suddenly everything became real. He found the inexplicable fear creeping up on him once more. All he could do was give it his best shot; if that wasn't good enough, then it would be no fault of his own. Even so...

Monday lunchtime soon rolled around, and Jason found Dave chewing his lip in frustration upon his return to the Music block.

Jason was scheduled for a quiet hour and had rather been looking forward to marking this morning's work, leaving him free later to practice a new piece for his slot the following Thursday at Fats: Mondays could be quite productive if he was in the right frame of mind. Those plans rapidly halted.

WHEN THE SAX MAN PLAYS PART 1 MAKING IT

"What am I going to do?" Dave wrung his hands. "I can't even tune the guitar, never mind play in front of a crowd!"

"You'll be fine." Jason pressed him into a seat, sitting opposite him. He knew this would happen, sooner or later, in fact he quite expected it from every member of Miracle at some point.

Dave shook his head. "You don't understand." He took a deep shaky breath. "Kipper wants us to play, separately. He reckons we can play with Miracle, and by ourselves." He saw horror sweep Jason's expression. "Exactly! I can't do it!"

Jason took a deep breath, quashing the feeling that he *knew* something like this would happen. Hamish's words echoed around his head like a storm warning: *'he's trouble that one'*.

"Dave, you *can* do it. You've progressed far quicker than even I anticipated." He paused, sure that Dave was taking in his words of encouragement. "The fact that you can't tune the guitar is no problem, don't dwell on it. As for playing two songs, that's simple, you just practice twice as much. You know my motto."

"The more I practice, the better I am." Dave nodded, feeling slightly calmer. "Yes, but I don't know that I can deal with *him*. Can you imagine the power trip he'll be on?" Dave moaned, putting his head in his hands.

"You'll be fine - I'll give you some earplugs." Jason joked, pleased to see him smile. "But you can't have just the two of you? Who will sing? What will you play?"

"He reckons it's 'in hand'." Dave sighed.

"You've survived this far." Jason gave him an encouraging

smile. "You'll be fine, and I'm glad you're not leaving us."

"That was the point I argued. We made a promise. He could argue black and blue, but he admitted defeat this time."

"Quite a Miracle." Jason chuckled at his own irony.

WHEN THE SAX MAN PLAYS PART 1 MAKING IT
Chapter 5

Kipper thought over his conversation with the four lovely ladies he'd met for lunch. They had commiserated with him over the overruling of his song choice. What they had misheard through the rumour-mill, Kipper ensured he spun the tale stronger, and more in his favour, playing Jason as a tyrant in disguise.

From then, Georgie's opinion of him changed considerably. Not that Kipper noticed; too wrapped up in their deliberate flattery, unaware that they were buttering him up to agree with their idea. He accepted their proposal, concurring that having a gorgeous front-girl would win vital votes.

Georgie had been done up to the nines for this meeting and felt silly, but had Leanne's and Sophie's hands clamping her to her seat as if she might run away mid conversation.

Some twenty minutes later, after arrangements were made, Kipper left the ladies to their gossiping - sure that they would be talking about him, such was his inflated ego. On his way home, he wondered which one of them would be his first conquest, planning to woo all four. The very idea made his smile widen.

Georgie breathed a sigh of relief as he disappeared. She hoped Jason knew what suffering she was putting herself through for the cause, laughing at herself for having such a ridiculous thought.

"C'mon then, let's go!" Anna tugged on her arm, snapping her from her thoughts.

Georgie frowned. "Go where?"

Leanne and Sophie rolled their eyes, mock sighing.

"Shopping, Georgie!" Anna laughed.

Georgie shook her head. "Extra study session, can't tonight."

"Tough." Leanne took her arm, with Sophie taking her other arm, propelling her out of the building. "It wouldn't take long. Besides it'll be fun."

Georgie cringed, aware that she had no choice in the matter. She hated shopping. When she found trousers she liked, she bought three, sometimes in different colours. (Her version of 'different colours' were black, grey, brown and midnight blue.) Her wardrobe was sensible: (Leanne called it boring) suits, jumpers, plain tops, one pair of jeans and one pair of shorts for the summer. She kept away from the shopping centres, visiting the smaller out-of-town stores when necessary. This would be an absolute disaster, she felt sure.

Ten minutes later, Georgie stared at the rail of clothing, wearing an expression bordering horror. She felt sure everyone in the store could feel her hesitation. This had to be one killer outfit, in Leanne's words; sexy, smart and practical, Sophie had added; stage perfect, fun and sparkly, Anna had insisted.

Georgie seriously had to rock if there was any chance of reaching the Final. But what the hell was 'rock' and, more importantly, how would she carry it off?

Georgie saw the look pass between her girlfriends as Sophie produced the notebook; that excited, knowing look. Every page

contained a different famous woman, not all of them Georgie
recognised, each woman dressed entirely differently.

She was dragged off to a nearby coffee shop, sandwiched
between Leanne and Sophie while Anna ordered their usual
drinks as they waded through the photos, comments and
descriptions. Twenty minutes later, they dragged a still-reluctant
Georgie back to the shops in pursuit of their image of perfection.

Bewildered, Georgie stood back while the three grabbed their
ideal items, thrusting them into her arms. Then they shepherded
her to the changing room, demanding a modelling of everything
before snapping back the curtain.

Finally, Georgie had a chance to draw breath in peace. She
could hear her friends arguing over which outfit was best; which
was most practical; which was *perfect!* - and why. Really and
truly, she was thankful for their planning, knowing she couldn't
do it without their help.

Turning, she reviewed the assembled outfits. Leather trousers
and silver sparkly vest. Miniskirt and silk blouse. Floor-length
gown, in her favourite colour: purple. Georgie was a jeans-and-
t-shirt girl on her casual days; her version of dressing up was a
smart trouser suit and printed top, black shoes and bag; minimal
jewellery and virtually no make-up. She wore her dark brown
shoulder-length hair in a ponytail. This was her vision of hell, if
she allowed herself to admit it. But she was determined that she
would have fun, even if it killed her!

Which would she try first? She felt an inward rebellion against all three choices. Taking a deep breath, she removed her 'boring' clothes. Forcing herself to smile, she reminded herself that this was her only chance to see how her opposite life could be: it was her chance to have fun; to rebel against her serious nature and that of her family. She hardly dared hope that she would win Jason's heart, realising that she was starting to fall for the musical mystery man.

   This should be fun, Anna's words echoed in her head. Georgie knew Anna was right, her friend was right most of the time... She chose the dress first, carefully unwrapping the straps from the hanger, and unzipping the side fastening before stepping into the dress. Catching sight of herself in the mirror, she groaned.

"What's wrong?" Leanne asked, whipping the curtain open, Sophie and Anna close behind her.

"I have no cleavage!" Georgie's expression was tearful.

"Don't worry, I'll find you an asset-manager." Anna winked at her. She was gone before Georgie could blink.

"Nice." Leanne was sizing her up. "But too fancy, don't you think?" She looked at Sophie, who nodded.

"Feminine," she began, "beautiful colour though - suits those cheekbones." She pinched Georgie's cheeks before her hands were playfully slapped away.

"I want to see the leather next." Leanne gave her a bright smile, pulling the curtain over once more.

Georgie admired herself once more in the mirror, before carefully removing the dress and rehanging it. Unclipping the leather trousers, she was first appalled at the thought, but... this had to be the softest leather ever! It was gorgeous!

Her smile broadened as she stepped into the trousers, finding the fastening sat rather well - flat against her flat stomach, Leanne commented jealously. The sparkly vest was soft against her skin, and hugged her slim figure. Again the cleavage problem struck, but by then Anna had returned - with a bra that looked like a monstrosity! Georgie struggled to get it properly on, but when she did, the effect was amazing.

"It's called a balcony bra, to give you a lift." Anna nodded when Georgie emerged from the changing room and performed a mini-catwalk for her friends. "Every woman should have one!" Leanne snorted. "Some of us don't need that sort of help."

"Not all of us are as perfect as you." Anna retorted, winking at Georgie who looked a little disappointed by Leanne's comment. "I like this outfit better."

"You would!" Sophie laughed. "It's your choice!" She smiled at Georgie. "Now try the skirt and blouse, so we can compare." Georgie hesitated, being forced back into the changing room. Five long minutes later, she re-emerged, shaking her head. A sharp intake of breath from her friends proved they thought the same.

Leanne shook her head. "Shame. It's a damn sexy get-up."

"Sexy?" Sophie repeated, her eyes wide. "Siren, you mean!"

Anna too was horrified. The miniskirt was far too revealing. "I like the blouse though - nice colour, enhances marvellously." She

looked up at Georgie. "Swap the skirt for the trousers."
Sophie and Leanne beside her pulled faces, but Anna waved
Georgie back into the changing room. She nodded to herself
when Georgie came out, pleased that her idea had worked.

Georgie too seemed rather pleased with the choice, which was
a bonus considering it was her that would be wearing it.

"Still a little preppy." Leanne shook her head, getting to her feet.

"What're you doing?" Panic crept into Georgie's voice as
Leanne undid a few of the top buttons on the blouse.

"You need sex appeal, or you'll never win." Leanne frowned.
"Great bra," she muttered, making Anna grin. "Too good to hide
away." She stepped back to admire her handiwork, nodding to
herself. "Yes. We have a winner." She grinned at Georgie,
stepping forward again to embrace her. "Put your tomboy
clothes back on, we're going shoe shopping!"

Ten minutes later, Georgie shuddered. Stilettos gave her
nightmares just from looking at them. She couldn't understand
how women managed to walk in them for two minutes, never
mind lasted hours on them.

"I can still do boots, right?" Inspiration struck as she recalled
the pictures in the notebook. "Black polished leather, shiny silver
buckles, killer heels." She added for good measure, just to show
her friends how serious she was.

"Listen to you, you sound like a shoe freak!" Sophie chuckled.
Georgie too laughed. "I rather like the sound of that."
The four, in agreement, set off towards the boot section of the

footwear department, ooh-ing and ahh-ing over a multitude of styles, before Georgie put her foot down - literally. She tried three pairs, deciding on the most comfortable, arguing that she'd be wearing them for hours; throwing in the excuse that she couldn't possibly dance in anything higher.

Actually, dancing as part of the routine hadn't crossed her mind until that second. Georgie swallowed hard. The judges had warned 'stiff and starchy performances would be penalised', and so, Georgie was thankful for those dance classes her friends had pressed her into attending. She realised then that she would need her friends' help all the way.

And in the future? What if she and Jason hit it off? What would she do? What would she say? She knew her friends held the answers to these key questions - they were indispensable!

Chapter 6

"Would you mind?" Kipper paused for Jason's reaction.

It was cheeky to use the Music facilities when he was technically fighting against Jason, but anything was worth a try. He was also going to send Georgie in his direction for instruction and confidence-boosting, once he got Jason's agreement to hold the practice sessions there.

"I stay late on Mondays." Jason began, noting Kipper's expectant expression. "My classes don't finish until five."

"Five is fine. We can wait for the lesson to finish, it doesn't matter if you overrun." Kipper was aware this sort of conversation could be classed as desperate, but he needed the music man's influence - or rather, Dave and Georgie did.

Jason hid his smile, realising that Kipper going back on his word was a rare occurrence. A strange sense of satisfaction and worth filled him. He nodded. "Deal." He paused. "Will you let me review your entry?" He watched Kipper balk. "I need to know what it is if I'm to help. I take it that's your plan?"

"That would be great, thanks." Kipper swallowed hard, his tongue tripping over the words. He realised Jason was a good guy, he wasn't sure if their roles were reversed *he*'d be saying this to *himself.*

Jason smiled. There was no time to think about the day he'd had: he was on in less than ten minutes. He'd relax into playing mode the second his name was announced; he always did. What Jason hadn't counted on was knowing his audience, and by his audience he wasn't including the Club's usual clientele: Georgie and her girlfriends were there; and Michael lurked in the shadows, determined to only stay for Jason's piece and not distract him.

As usual, the place rocked to the sound of applause when Jason finished, including some wolf-whistles from the girls' table. Jason bowed to his admirers, blushing, raising his free hand in gesture as he left the stage.

He never let his saxophone out of his sight - it was something onlookers found amusing as Jason never went anywhere without the instrument. He returned to the room with the case in his hand, not five minutes later, heading to his usual table where his friends, Louis, James and Smith were. As he made his way across the room, he glanced at the four girls who'd paid him so much attention he'd almost forgotten what to play. Fortunately his music came so easily, so automatically, else his performance would have died.

As ever, his three friends were keen to hear his news and duly wanted an update on the band's progress. Jason had already been badgered into providing tickets for them *for every stage.* That was confidence if ever he heard it. Every session at Fats was good for him in so many ways. The buzz performing gave him; the support from his companions and the advice they dealt at the drop of a hat; the sense of belonging instilled into him: their vote of confidence was the cherry on the top of the cake.

A voice broke the comfortable silence around the table.

"Would you like to join us for a celebratory drink?" Leanne's sultry tone raised a few eyebrows around the table.

"Who's celebrating?" Jason turned to her, smiling.

"All of us." She paused, flirting with her *whole body*, Jason realised with shock.

He was nudged on both sides, loud accusations of "needing to let go every so often" flying around the table. Almost reluctantly he allowed himself to be led across the room, trying to stop the blush creeping up his neck. He spotted his new protégée, Georgie, in the middle, looking slightly uncomfortable.

"What a performance!" Anna congratulated him. "I had no idea you were so good!"

Jason thanked her, realising the young lady who'd accosted him was now at the bar. Sophie and Georgie were both nodding in agreement. Jason couldn't help noticing the pairs of wine glasses littering the small circular table. What was it that made students and drinking go so well together?

He hoped to make a quick exit before something happened, realising he had to be a credible character in front of Georgie. Her so-called 'raw talent' had turned out not so bad, and the song was well-constructed with her in mind. His memory went back a few days when Georgie's Guys had turned up for their first practice session, where Georgie's song "Say What You Want" had overridden Kipper's choice. Worse was to come for

Kipper, as Georgie too was adamant that Jason play with them;
the thought sent steam pouring from Kipper's ears.

Jason had only allowed himself to laugh when the trio had left
later that night. The memory made him want to laugh even now.
After sharing a drink and idle chatter with the group, he excused
himself to return to his friends, glad to escape to relative safety!

Dave again was waiting for him on the following Tuesday, this
time it was early evening just as Jason was making plans to
leave. One look at the crestfallen young man in front of him
changed his mind.

"I really tried to believe you," he began, not daring to look up.
"I really tried to keep the two bands separate..."

"No-one said it was going to be easy." Jason began.

Dave shuddered, looking around. "Can we go somewhere else
to talk?"

Jason was bemused by this; however, his mind immediately
presented an image of the Union Bar. Dave nodded to his
suggestion and Jason wondered what was behind his negative
attitude, that it was more than he was just overwhelmed by the
new experiences opening up in front of him.

At Friday's practice session, Jason handed every band member
a pen, pointing to the chart, which answered the questioning
looks as to why Georgie had arrived at their practice - Michael
and Vince had heard of her but not actually met her, until now.

WHEN THE SAX MAN PLAYS PART 1 MAKING IT

Everyone's name was on the board, alongside the days of the week, the header was "Commitment To Practice".

Georgie's Guys had just entered before the deadline, being placed last. This worked well for Jason as it meant their first March audition was on Friday 6th at 8 pm - the audition for Miracle was at 7.30 pm, Wednesday 4th.

Jason knew he would have to place band activity before his usual performance at Fats on Thursday nights - after all, he was asking everyone else to change their activities to fit, so he had to follow the same rule himself.

"We don't want overkill." Jason paused, standing in front of the white board with pen in hand. "Practice three times a week should suffice." He sighed. "Thanks to someone, that doubles my workload." He shot Kipper a dirty look, though managing also to radiate innocence.

Everyone in the room detected a serious undercurrent to his teasing tone, and a few muffled laughs broke out.

Dave smiled at Jason, whom he held in even higher regard since their private conversation a few days previously. "I can work around my commitment."

Kipper snorted. "I can't!"

"I can have change accommodated for me." Jason admitted, placing a cross on a Thursday. "Being a creature of habit I don't want to change, but if needs must." He shrugged, turning to Kipper. "Why don't you mark your busy days next?"

Kipper got up, eyeing Jason's dots on other days apart from

WHEN THE SAX MAN PLAYS PART 1 MAKING IT

Thursday. Well... Friday nights were busiest: he crossed Friday.
Sunday nights were his prep nights: he crossed Sunday.
Wednesday was always an important night for him, all the parties
were on Wednesdays and Saturdays: he crossed Wednesday
and Saturday out.

Jason gave a snort of indignation. "That's your commitment, you
can pledge Mondays, Tuesdays and Thursdays?"

The irony in Jason's voice was lost to Kipper, who'd been
struck by another thought: Mondays were busy with weekend
replenishment. He crossed Monday.

"Get out!" Jason hissed.

"What?" Kipper's attention returned to the present. It never
struck him *why* everyone in the room was looking at him in
horror. To him the world was a stage, and he was a player:
therefore holding the room's attention was his aim.

"GET OUT!" Jason raged, striding to the door and flinging it
open. His body shook with anger, making his outstretched finger
tremble.

Kipper huffed, and took two steps towards the door, hesitating.
Jason continued: "Think about your priorities! DON'T come
back until *YOU* can fit US in!!" He slammed the door behind
him.

The two groups looked at each other in the ugly silence,
knowing this wasn't the first time Kipper had been ejected, each
secretly wondering whether he'd return.

Jason eyed the rest of the group. "Who's next? And I'm warning you all, I won't stand for a repeat performance of *that*!"

"Definitely not!" Michael exclaimed, looking around him. "I can work round anything." He smiled at Jason, glad to find him calmer. To prove his point, he dotted all seven days.

"Ditto." Georgie said quietly. "I have a mountain of work but I'll just rearrange my schedule, it's no problem. I want to be here." She too smiled at Jason, dotting all seven days.

Nervousness threatened to swamp Vince: he swallowed hard. "We're at the beginning of the wedding season." His gaze dropped to the floor.

"I do understand." Jason replied calmly. "That's why I wanted to do this so that we can be honest with each other. There are only so many hours in the day. What are your busy times?" Everyone followed Vince's shaky hand as he crossed Friday, Saturday and Sunday, but dotted the rest.

"That's okay." Jason tried to soothe. "Don't worry, we all have something we can't change, whether it's work or play." His gaze then fell on Dave. "What's your busiest time?"

"I have seven-day auctions." Dave said quietly. "On Fridays."

"So Fridays are crossed out for most of us. I'll change to a Friday, to fit in." Jason smiled at the still nervous group.

"Are you sure?" Georgie said softly. "You've played Thursdays for..." she paused. "A long time, I don't know how long." Jason smiled, wondering for a fleeting moment if she'd been doing some homework on him. It was sweet if she had. He found that he was developing a soft spot for her - already!

WHEN THE SAX MAN PLAYS PART 1 MAKING IT

"Four years." Michael spoke.

Jason's mouth fell open. Obviously, someone had been doing their homework. He *had* wondered if he was imagining that Michael was rather friendly towards him, but now he knew it wasn't his imagination. Inwardly, he swore.

WHEN THE SAX MAN PLAYS PART 1 MAKING IT
Chapter 7

It had been a rough weekend, Jason shook his head with his thoughts. He was glad to be in the security of the College, specifically in the Music block, sinking into his usual chair.

Automatically he switched the kettle on, letting his thoughts run. To top it all off, he had Georgie's Guys tonight. It wasn't their fault they were raw and nervous, and having Kipper there also would cause havoc he felt sure.

He sunk his head into his hands, events of the past 56 hours rolling again through his memory. His Friday night slot at Fats was a disaster. His piece had gone well, and he'd met his friends as normal; shared their normal conversations and laughs. His equilibrium had been fully restored when the woman had appeared.

Firstly, she congratulated him on his performance, placing a glass in front of him before getting up to do her set of love songs, all dedicated to him: Jason's face flamed.

He usually walked home from Fats, as Thursdays were quiet where he lived. Fridays were a nightmare to navigate with people spilling from pubs and clubs everywhere he turned. He couldn't believe the difference twenty four hours made, soon realising it wasn't quite as safe a neighbourhood as he thought, deciding to take a cab the short ride home.

He jumped into a taxi just as a group of burly drunks behind him started fighting, counting his blessings. He was more than surprised when the blonde woman from Fats hopped into the other side, waving the driver on. Speechless, he stared at her. She talked at him for the duration of the journey, non-stop.

Upon arrival at his flat, she got out with him, pressing him up the stairs. Jason wondered how he was going to get rid of her, determined not to open the door while she was still there.

A yell from the street interrupted his thoughts. The man looked frighteningly like one of those fighting drunks he'd left a few blocks behind - and he was bellowing at him. The blonde pressed herself further into Jason, yelling back at him. Jason's muddled brain couldn't comprehend the conversation, catching only snatches: she was leaving him for a real man; someone who didn't fix things by killing those who stood in his way.

Killing? Jason's eyes widened in horror. His brain kicked in that instant, seeing the man had followed them in another taxi, which was waiting no doubt for payment.

Jason bounded down the steps, the blonde following him. The drunkard grabbed his girlfriend with one hand, swinging a punch at Jason with his free hand, catching him in the face. Hugging the sax case to him, safe in the refuge of the cab, speeding away from the trouble outside his own flat, his mind turned to his brother and his safe haven in Kensington.

"Alright, guv? Where to?" The driver asked.

Still shaking, Jason had automatically rattled off Christopher's address, nursing his throbbing head.

Christopher's words rolled around his mind. *It was an*

isolated incident. It won't happen again. But if he needed to return, he could, anytime.

The thought of moving was perhaps his only option. He wondered for a moment if this was an overreaction on his part, not entirely convinced... A sudden, sharp knock on the door made him jump. The door opened, although he hadn't actually answered it.

"I'm sorry, I just wanted to say that I'm a complete... what the hell happened to you?!" Kipper put his head round the door and seeing the state Jason was in, let himself into the room.

Jason waved him away. "Doesn't matter."

"Oh." Kipper stopped.

Jason looked up at him, seeing the hesitation in Kipper's expression. "You're a complete idiot and you've decided to pledge us some of your precious time. Is that what you're saying?"

"Not quite my choice of words." Kipper laughed, hoping to raise a small smile from the ashen-faced man opposite him.

"I'm sorry, I don't want to talk - are you finished?" Jason killed their conversation before it had properly begun.

"I'm sorry, I'm a complete..."

Jason cut him off. "Yes, yes, I understand; grovel, grovel." He shook his head. "I accept your apology - try to engage your brain next time. I know it's hard."

Kipper nodded, wondering if Jason was going to continue.

"See you later."

WHEN THE SAX MAN PLAYS PART 1 MAKING IT

Kipper stood up, still hesitating.

"Close the door behind you." Jason added, sighing when the door closed very quietly behind Kipper.

"I feel like a car manufacturer." Jason quipped, having written M-G M-G M-G across his diary in the Monday, Tuesday, Wednesday, Thursday, Saturday, Sunday spaces.

"You haven't got the hands of a mechanic." Georgie spoke gently, having been informed of the morning's conversation with Kipper.

Everyone had, and was on tenterhooks for the day. Miracle had come along to Georgie's Guys practice, having heard the news.

"Thank God." Michael replied. "How would you play?"

"ANYway." Jason spoke loudly, aware that he was going to lose their collective concentration unless he interrupted now. "Why are you lot here? This isn't your practice."

"We wanted to offer you our support." Vince began. "In whatever way we can." He looked at Jason meaningfully. "If you want to combine the two sessions, then we're fine with that." He continued quickly. "Actual group combination would be difficult, but I thought we could practice in separate rooms? Kipper and Dave can flit between us. I know I'd welcome the extra practice." He looked around him, pleased to get nods of agreement and encouraging smiles. "And, well, if you want to bounce something off us, we're here." He received another round of nods and smiles, turning to Jason for his reaction.

"Thanks." Jason paused, and everyone could see how touched he was. "That might work. It might be hard for these guys." He indicated Kipper and Dave. "But hey, we don't know unless we try, so why not?" He gave them a small smile.

Georgie nodded. So what if she was left alone with Jason? A small shiver of pleasurable apprehension rolled over her. Solo practice was no problem in her mind.

They would pursue their friendship, she read the vibes that he gave off in her company - he liked her. She knew he would keep the relationship professional, but once she'd graduated... you didn't know what was around the corner, Anna kept telling her. Her friends told her the signs she was to look out for, and Jason was displaying most of them.

"Starting with you lot." Jason looked at Miracle. "You can set yourselves up by now, can't you? Everything's ready, so off you go." His gaze briefly settled on Dave, the two of them sharing their secret. "I hope you don't mind being left alone?" Jason's eyebrows raised as he spoke, Georgie noticed.

"No." She tried to keep the tremor out of her voice, following him to the smaller room where they'd met in last week.

"Do you know your words?"

Georgie shook her head. "Not quite yet. I know the chorus, obviously." She laughed, nervously.

Jason too laughed. "Don't worry, you'll be fine. The more you practice, the more you will absorb."

"Like a sponge?" She joked.

WHEN THE SAX MAN PLAYS PART 1 MAKING IT

"If you like." Jason laughed, placing a music stand in front of her. "I'll just collect the sax and check on the guys, then I'm all yours." He winced at his choice of words, hurrying out of the room, desperately hoping she wouldn't think he was flirting with her. He was struck then by the realisation that *actually* that *was* what he was doing.

"I know what you mean." She said to his retreating back, alas out of his earshot.

Five minutes later, he re-entered the room, looking harassed, apologising to her. She watched him take the saxophone from it's protective case, automatically rigging it to that little clip and sling that went around his neck. Fleetingly, she was jealous of the instrument being that close to him. She shut out the thought, turning her mind to the music.

They ran through the song twice before Jason left again to check on Miracle. Not a minute later, he put his head around the door, beckoning her into the next room.

"We're going to run through the whole song. I want you to listen and tell us what you think - as an outsider, with a musical ear." He winked at her. "Feel free to say we're crap, okay?"

They both laughed, but the rest of the group were horrified.

"Don't say that." Dave whispered, swallowing hard.

"Ah c'mon," Georgie grinned at him, "you're not crap - you've got more talent than I have in my little finger!"

Jason sent her a silent thank you, having momentarily forgotten Dave's sensitivity. Perhaps another pep talk was around the corner?

"We need to practice, to get away from the roughness of a band's first performance together. No-one said it will be easy." He warned. "Count us in please Georgie, to three."

Coming in for Wednesday's practice session, two days later, Georgie frowned. "Your face looks worse."

Gently she held his face in her hands. This close, he could smell her perfume. He retained a grip on his senses, aware that it would be easy to... *It's friendly concern that's all*, he told himself.

Yet, his mind reeled with the possibility that it was more. He shook his head with his thoughts; Georgie let go of him.

He smiled at her. "It's fine. Bruising always looks worse before it disappears."

She was still frowning. "You should put something on it."

"I've been using the frozen peas trick."

"No Arnica?"

Jason frowned. "That herbal gel? I've heard it doesn't work."

Georgie rolled her eyes. "You won't know unless you try. Honestly! You men, you're all the same; you need a good woman to look after you." She fussed with the song sheet, hoping that Jason hadn't seen the look in her eyes. She hadn't meant to say that - her face reddened at the thought of coming onto him so blatantly.

"Maybe." Jason murmured, also preparing for their practice,

laying out music sheets by Kipper's keyboard and Dave's guitar, pre-tuned, as per their secret agreement.

Tonight was the night he would give Dave extra time, trying to teach him to tune the guitar; trying to tune his stubborn tone deaf ears. Jason felt this was the reason behind his lack of confidence - or at least one of them.

Despite Georgie's best efforts, his saxophone didn't fit with her music choice. Dave's confidence in both guitar and drums did not exist, and Vince refused to commit himself to two bands, citing he was too busy. Thus Jason swapped his saxophone for drums, having had a few private practices before taking the decision. The drummer was the heart of the band; it was an important responsibility and one he was determined not to ruin through lack of practice.

It was now three weeks until Miracle's audition, and a further two days until Georgie's Guys were subjected to the same panel: Jason's nerves were already jangling. His worst nightmare was falling at the first hurdle. Would Fate be so cruel?

Chapter 8

That weekend Georgie called the girls to an emergency meeting:
the aim - to blitz her wardrobe. She had her performance outfit,
but none of her usual bland clothes stretched to the requirements
of band practice. Her three friends shared a grin: Georgie was
hooked!

They plugged her for insider information: how was the band
doing? What realistically was their chance? What was Jason
really like? Did he like her too? Smiling, Georgie answered their
questions, confiding that there was definitely something between
them, describing how he'd shaken her off a few days ago - and
she'd only been examining his black eye! Sophie and Leanne
shared a dirty look, which Georgie laughed off.

"Are you sure that's all you were doing?" Anna teased.
Sophie stopped walking, putting her arm around her friend's
shoulders. "You've definitely got him!" She winked at Georgie,
who's face began to flame.

Desperately Georgie wondered how she was going to change
the conversation, especially as she'd started it! What would
happen if a relationship *did* blossom between her and Jason?

She imagined he would make a wonderful lover: caring,
attentive, unselfish... She shook her head with her thoughts. She
couldn't allow herself to think such things, not before she knew
that they weren't unfounded. She changed the subject. "I need
practical outfits, that's all. Something comfortable but stylish."

WHEN THE SAX MAN PLAYS PART 1 MAKING IT

For once she was glad to be in the heart of the shopping district; relieved to find her instinct to trust her friends had been correct.

Two hours later, all four were loaded up with bags; each girl had had her say, and Georgie had taken onboard all their advice. Tired but happy, she made her way home, promising to meet up the day after for their Sunday night ritual, in the Union Bar after practice.

Georgie realised she wouldn't be at all surprised to find her friends creep into the Music block to listen at the door! In a funny way, she realised that she would actually like it if they did.

She kept seeing those famous women cut-outs in her mind's eye. They all looked perfect; no flaws, no imperfections. Every morning and evening now, she studied her reflection in the simple bathroom mirror - could she look that interesting; that beautiful? Sophie had said about having something done with her hair, but Georgie had been too frightened to take the offer up. Staring at her reflection, she wondered if now was the time to bite the bullet...

Miracle were, of course, the most polished of the two bands. That was to be expected, Jason pointed out; they had been practising for longer and had more time together to bond.

Kipper and Dave already had that bond, and Georgie wondered if she should make more of an effort to bond with *them*. With that thought in the forefront of her mind, she invited them - as well as Miracle - to share a few drinks with her friends before another busy College week.

She realised her mistake as Leanne got hold of Jason. His quiet personality clashed awfully with Leanne's, so Georgie did the first thing that came to her mind to rescue him - sitting between the pair. The audible relief across Jason's face made her giggle.

Vince found that Jason's words of encouragement were ringing true: the more they practised, the more confident they became. Guilt washed over him when he couldn't attend the first Sunday night practice, despite their assurances that it didn't matter. It did matter, Vince could not stress the point enough!

It was impossible for him to practice at home - a drum kit was less than portable! He liked the idea of joining Georgie's Guys for extra practice on Wednesdays, shutting himself away in the smaller room. Here, he discovered he played best with his eyes shut, for some bizarre reason.

Jason laughed when he shared this observation. "Whatever makes you feel better Vince, it doesn't matter how silly it seems. Did anyone ever tell you the public speaking secret?"

Vince's frown spoke volumes, so Jason continued.

"The way to diminish nerves in front of an audience is to imagine them in their underwear."

Vince laughed, feeling a weight lifted from his shoulders.

He was still smiling as he left the Music block an hour later, unaware of the young lady following him until she called his name. Vince turned, and smiled in recognition; she was in his

English class, his mind blanked on her name - then it struck him:
Ami Kelsey.

She was a pretty nineteen year old, who worked weeknights in
a bar, struggling to pay for her course. They walked home
together; the notion that she had been waiting for him not striking
Vince. It was strange that they lived in the same street, he was
sure that he hadn't seen her nearby before now. Ami explained
that she had recently changed digs; the explanation settling
Vince's questioning mind. They chatted about their families, their
ambitions, and Miracle, pausing as they arrived at Ami's flat.
She invited him in, besieging him with her large blue eyes. Vince
did not hesitate, smiling to think his plan was working already!

By Miracle's scheduled practice the following Monday, Vince
was head-over-heels in love with Ami. Kipper had landed the
lead in the month's new play, which was to be shown to the
College as a whole, an achievement he reminded everyone of at
every opportunity. He bragged also about his relationship with
the leading lady, especially how she couldn't resist his charms.

Jason shook his head in disbelief. He knew it was February;
the time that normal people lost their minds to their fanciful
notions of the three L's: love, lust and longing - and not just on
the 14th day of the month!

Vince and Kipper were besotted... and he had two band
members vying for his attention. This wouldn't be so bad if they
were both female. *Alas we cannot choose our circumstances -*

WHEN THE SAX MAN PLAYS PART 1 MAKING IT

Christopher's favourite phrase stuck in Jason's mind. It was so apt!

Jason sighed, heavily. Georgie was a wonderful girl; articulate, talented and down-to-earth, almost his vision of perfect - apart from the fact she was a student! Christopher had warned him about the young ladies at Impervious, sure that more than a few would fall for his naive brother when they got to know him.

Except, nobody had counted on Michael's obvious crush. The youngster hung off Jason's every word. Jason found himself scanning the crowd at Fats for his shadow on Fridays, knowing he was there, despite his best intentions to keep hidden. He tried to feel flattered, but failed, only worrying.

Worse still, he wondered how Michael would react to any extra attention in Georgie's direction. Jealousy was a dangerous thing.

WHEN THE SAX MAN PLAYS PART 1 MAKING IT
Chapter 9

Jason had wondered if it had been a sign, looking back. Vince had not appeared for his extra practice session, but worryingly, neither had he appeared the following night for his scheduled band practice. Undoubtedly it was due to the new love of his life.

Jason sighed exasperatedly. Miracle were starting to look and act like a polished band; this was not how it was meant to be - not with ten days to go before the qualification auditions!

The storage room - containing many guitars and keyboards, plectrums, lecterns and other accessories - also hosted the back up drum kit Vince was becoming accustomed to. Jason sat heavily on the circular stool, picking up the discarded drumsticks. He glanced across the hall, as if to his abandoned saxophone, pausing for thought before starting to bash out a rhythm.

His first class of the morning had obediently sat at their places in the room next door, the din distant to their ears through the soundproofed walls. Two students got up ten minutes later, soon finding Jason locked in his trance in the next room. No amount of shouting and hand waving would attract his attention, as his eyes were closed in concentration.

The bravest of the two students took tentative steps towards his tutor, edging yet closer, ducking out of the way of the flying drumsticks. Just as he was about to tap him on the shoulder,

Jason became aware of their presence, snapping from his higher plain and scaring the hell out of the two students in the room.

That evening Vince answered his phone dreamily, also high on another plain. Jason's angry tone soon brought him down to Earth with a thump: he'd been so wrapped up in the intimacy of one man and one woman...

Ami was nowhere to be seen, he realised as he woke up properly. He hadn't left the bed for the last 48 hours, except to bring back food and drink. He padded to the bathroom when the call ended, a smile lighting his face to find her in the shower. In a flash, he joined her, Jason's words instantly forgotten.

Only in the small hours, in one of those snatched half-asleep conversations, he confessed to her his sin. Too fast, Ami was awake and sitting bolt upright. Vince realised there and then that he would do anything for this woman.

He was astonished by her anger; her arms crossed across her ample chest. His brain struggled to comprehend what she said. *She didn't want him if he wasn't in the band.*

The downward spiral sucked Vince into its dark depression as her words, and the realisation behind them, sunk in. It was just like a rerun of his childhood memories. His mother had the worst relationship history with a string of boyfriends, all using her to get what they wanted before leaving. One night he'd gone into her bedroom after a terrifying nightmare looking for comfort, as only a seven-year-old can do. He didn't know his mother was not alone and not asleep; worse still, the man she had bedded took one look at him and left immediately. Her sobbed words continued to haunt him: *nobody loves me because of you, nobody wants you!*

"Sack me," he spoke quietly, his gaze fixed to the floor, unable to look Jason in the eye the next morning.

"That'd be too easy." Jason spat, sensing something serious. "And it would make Miracle a complete laughing stock." He paused. "If we aren't already." He sighed. "What's going on?"

"It's all a complete mess." Vince's voice was hollow.

Jason studied his face, surprised to find the Vince so full of fire and so energetic that he'd come to know and rely on, so miserable. "Your girlfriend's left you, is that it?"

Vince shook his head sadly. "I don't want to talk about it."

"She has left you?" Jason probed gently.

"She only wanted me because of my attachment to the band." Vince sighed, sinking lower in his chair. "But it's not just that." He risked opening his eyes, peering timidly at Jason, who was sitting quietly opposite him, silently willing him to continue.

He spilled out the whole story - his broken home; the string of strangers he'd hoped would stay and be a father-figure to him; why he was so crap with girls; why he thought the band was his key to a better existence...

Jason cut in. "It *is* your key to a better existence. You make of life what you can. Experience teaches us so much, and it helps us learn about ourselves and about others." Jason paused for effect,

75

sure that he had Vince's attention. "We all make mistakes. You're a bright young man Vince; you have talent, perseverance and patience. You can succeed at anything you put your mind to. Love; work; life, whatever you want, only you can make it happen. Nobody else."

Vince nodded slowly, letting Jason's words roll around his mind.

"Did you work today?" Jason's question caught him unaware. Vince shook his head. "No, the wedding's off." He gave an ironic laugh. "But tomorrow's is still on."

Jason half-smiled. "Think about what I've said and we'll see you on Monday."

Vince nodded sheepishly, slinking out of the room with his tail between his legs.

"You're doing just fine." Jason smiled encouragingly at Georgie, ignoring the cute way she blushed. "But you need projection."

"Projection?" Kipper repeated.

Jason could see Dave wince out of the corner of his eye, and hid his smile. He got the impression that Dave sometimes regretted joining Kipper's mad plans. They were quite a duo.

"Yes, surely you've covered this in your acting classes. From the diaphragm, *project* your voice." He turned away from Kipper, who nodded, to Georgie. "Imagine: we're onstage when the lights go out and your microphone goes off - how are you going to reach the audience?"

Georgie gave him a look of hopelessness and Jason laughed,

plunging the room into darkness.

"Guys, I want you to play." Two small beams of light came from the ceiling, one over Kipper, one over Dave; the action making them laugh. "I'm going to sing, so no laughing. Georgie has to learn and sometimes the best way is by example."
Georgie could feel him moving around the room, stopping by her. He counted to three and the song began.

"Join in whenever you want to." Jason spoke in her ear.
Her body tingled as she felt his breath on her neck. He let her sing the chorus solo, urging her louder and louder still, urging her to feel the music from inside; from the diaphragm. He placed his hand gently on hers on her body, making her aware of the little-used muscle, causing fireworks to go off in her head at the magic of his touch. As she sang, he pressed her there, not hurting her, just encouraging her.

"Better!" They could all hear the smile in his voice as he spoke. "Good Georgie, good! I knew you could do it! Keep it going."
He gave them a round of applause at the finish of the second play, turning the lights back on and dazzling everyone in the room.

"Perfect!" He grinned at them. "We're as good as ready!"

An hour later, he fell into his chair at home tired but happy, a smile of satisfaction on his face. Not bad for a Friday! His eye fell on the time, and he shot out of the chair, collecting his sax on his way out, suddenly remembering his slot at Fats.

His companions, as usual, wanted all the details. They all shook their heads in sympathy when Jason recounted Vince's childhood woes, each thinking aloud the thoughts that echoed in Jason's mind. Would this affect Vince's performance from now on? Would he bounce back from the disastrous relationship, and the equally disastrous life he'd been brought into?

They were pleased to hear of the progress of Georgie's Guys, Georgie especially; teasing Jason that she was falling in love with him. He was consumed with shock: the notion of love had not crossed his mind.

Jason had never been in love. He'd heard plenty about the hurt and denial that happened when you fell out of love; how it blinkered you from reality; clouding your usually sane judgement; filling your world with happiness and togetherness.

They laughed at his uncomfortable state, reassuring him that love was a precious element in life. Pure love was the world's greatest strength, and the best thing that could happen to anyone. Jason did not believe these romantic, wistful words, already drowning in fear. Yes, love did not hurt if you found your soul mate, your Miss Right and turned her into Mrs Right. But how did you know if she was Miss Right Now but not Miss Right Forever? And once you knew the theories, how did you put them into practice?

WHEN THE SAX MAN PLAYS PART 1 MAKING IT
Chapter 10

Georgie sat beside him, nine days later, nervously awaiting
Miracle's curtain call. Dave looked positively sick and Kipper
kept nudging him, telling him to stop worrying.

"It's a breeze," Kipper boasted, laughing at the act that were
currently on. "They can't even sing!"

"Keep your voice down!" Jason hissed.

Kipper could be so insensitive at times, thanks to his inflated
ego. Hamish hadn't been wrong to express dismay at Kipper's
involvement in the band. When he'd heard Kipper had formed a
breakaway group, Hamish calmly told Jason that it would work
out for the best, if it was meant to. Even now, Jason couldn't
work out if that was a compliment or not.

"He's got a point. They're nothing on us." Georgie said quietly.

"Us?" Dave repeated, secretly glad to see that Michael looked
equally as sick as he felt.

"Both of us." Georgie grinned at him. "Our music is great;
they're crap."

Jason laughed, drawing in a deep breath as the group onstage
finished and polite clapping rippled around the room. "C'mon
guys, we're on." He picked up his saxophone, patting it fondly.
"Wish us luck, Georgie." His heart lifted when he saw how she
smiled at him.

He was looking forward to their audition in two days time, but
not as much as he was looking forward to this. Miracle was his

baby; his idea - the culmination of everyone's hard work and dedication to achieving the same shared dream. The idea of failing now... he didn't dare finish the thought, patting Dave encouragingly on the shoulder as he walked Michael to the centre of the stage, seeing the microphone shaking in his hand.

"Don't worry," Jason whispered to him, "just imagine you're at home with your dad and the record's coming on. We're all behind you."

In the darkness, Jason cringed at his choice of words, thankful that he hadn't said that *he* was behind him, sure that was part of Michael's fantasies about him. Oh yes, Jason hadn't been able to avoid hearing the rumours about his front man. He just hoped that post-performance jubilation wouldn't give Michael the courage to speak to him on that topic.

He swallowed hard, tapping his foot to the beat in his brain, counting them in. The lights came up and Vince began the intro, Jason followed his lead, happy to hear Kipper and Dave start perfectly alongside him. For a shocked second of silence, Michael did not sing. They all stopped playing, but Vince carried on, unaware of the dilemma. Jason grabbed his nearest hand, startling him, causing him to jump and crash a symbol. Everyone in the hall laughed - except the judging panel.

"What th...." Kipper's voice echoed in the quietness of the hall. Jason made a "zip it" motion to him, striding over to Michael, who was quite obviously in the throes of utter stage-fright. He gripped the youngster's shoulders, calming him, reviving his shaken confidence, getting him to nod after a moment or two that seemed to stretch out for an eternity.

"I'm sorry," Jason addressed the room, but more specifically the judges. "We're not used to a large crowd. Perhaps it'll be second time lucky."

"It better be." Jason heard one of the judges mutter.

Michael positively quaked.

Jason glanced sideways as Georgie mouthed something to him. He frowned, unsure of what she said. He saw her leave and returned to his own preparations. Seconds later, the lights went off again, to everyone's puzzlement. Jason smiled: Georgie had rigged the lights. Not knowing how long they had, he counted them in again. Vince began and he followed, then Kipper and Dave; the lights remained dark.

Taking a deep breath, Michael began, his quiet voice steadily growing in confidence, projecting into the room by the first chorus, much to the band's relief. The lights snapped on during the second verse - by then Michael was in full voice. The end of the song was characterised by Jason's sax solo, which was virtually drowned out by the roar of the assembled crowd.

Jason saw Hamish smiling and giving him a thumbs-up, but some of the panel were frowning. He ushered Miracle off the stage before anyone else saw.

Arriving at Impervious early the next morning, barely 12 hours since he'd left, Jason approached the General Notice board, sighting the stark white notice pinned there. Despite his early arrival, there was already a crowd surrounding the notice. The hubbub increased as he approached.

For a moment, Jason wondered... but yes, it was *the* list. The list of bands through to the next round from the previous evening. Butterflies of nerves erupted in his stomach as he drew near enough to read the names, seeing the bands were categorised not in order of play, nor in alphabetical order - but *in order of merit*. Jason exhaled sharply, unaware that he'd been holding his breath: Miracle had taken the top spot.

He turned around, seeing Kipper, Dave and Georgie also reading the results. All three wore the same grin; the same twinkle of triumph and excitement in their eyes. Kipper had ripped off a salute, army-style, and they'd all collapsed into laughter. The four had then gone their separate ways, knowing that practice would bring them together again this evening.

Just as Jason lost sight of the trio, Chambers passed him, muttering something inaudible. He was sure the lecturers would all be sadly disappointed this morning, deciding to have his afternoon coffee in the staff room to indulge in some gloating.

Then Michael arrived. Theatrically, he screwed his eyes closed, protesting that he didn't want to know. He'd spent the night grovelling and apologising; convinced that he'd ruined it for everyone. No amount of cajoling would dispel such thoughts from his mind, and they'd given up, knowing their Fate was in the hands of the judges. Jason's mind kept showing the scene of the judges frowning while Hamish smiled, beginning to think maybe Michael's premonition would come true; consoling himself with the thought that he had a second chance with Georgie's Guys. Now, he hoped that they would have an equally successful night, but only time would tell.

"I can't look!" Michael moaned, his hands over his eyes.

"You must." Jason insisted, smiling at him when Michael peeked between his fingers, his face filling with delight.

"First?" He repeated, unable to believe his eyes.

Jason nodded. "Thanks to you."

"No," Michael shook his head vigourously, "thanks to *you*, you're the talent."

"We all have talent, and we work well together as a band." Jason smiled at him. "You'd better get going, classes start in a minute. See you on Monday."

Michael frowned. "You're cancelling practice?"

"You don't need practice." Jason laughing, patting him on the shoulder. "Besides it's the other audition on Friday."

His hand flew to his mouth. "How could I forget? I'll be there."

"Okay." Jason smiled to himself, knowing this would be his response. "I'm sure Dave and Georgie will appreciate the moral support."

Michael nodded and turned away, heading to his morning class. Jason took a deep breath and headed down the now deserted corridors to his awaiting morning class.

The trio awaiting him that evening radiated nerves. Well, Dave and Georgie were; Kipper was still buzzing from the success of their previous performance, Jason could see.

"Guys, you need to put last night's experience to one side in your mind. We cannot allow ourselves to become complacent. Miracle's qualification doesn't mean we will automatically qualify tomorrow."

"We know that." Kipper rolled his eyes.

"Have you seen the opposition?" Jason produced a play list, dated Friday 6th March. Georgie saw it was a long list, and there were hand-written additions scrawled on the bottom.

At first, she wondered what sort of tactic this was that Jason was using. Now she felt fear bite her. But if Miracle got through, then they would also: essentially they were the same group. That second, it struck her that she was looking forward to performing, and winning. She was struck by the desire to succeed; to win over her audience; to tease winning votes from the harsh judges.

"We should watch tonight's auditions."

The same puzzled look crossed between the three, but they followed Jason, creeping quietly into the back row of seating in the hall. They sat quietly for half an hour, spellbound by the talent on display.

"What happened?" Kipper hissed. "They put us in with the crap ones?!"

Several people turned around, shooting them quietening looks. Jason shrugged.

Georgie moaned, drawing their attention to the stage: the current group were performing her song. Worse still, their *gorgeous* leading lady had a *fabulous* voice. Her eyes were riveted to the stage, even as Dave dragged her out with Kipper and Jason not far behind, trying make sense of what she was burbling between floods of tears.

"Georgie, don't be silly." Jason sat down on the brick wall edging on the stairway beside her, not daring to touch her. "We can't change the song now. And anyway, it doesn't matter that another band is doing the same song."

"It doesn't?" Dave asked, squatting beside them.

Jason shook his head. "If it comes to it, we'll go head-to-head in the final qualifier, before the Quarterfinals."

"And we'd win." Kipper stated.

Jason looked up at him, thankful then for his total confidence in self and band.

"We wouldn't." Georgie sniffed.

"Of course we would!" Kipper grinned at her. "We have major talent number one," he indicated Jason with a flourish, "with your fabulous voice, Dave and I have the charm to take it to the top!"

Dave blushed and Jason tried not to laugh.

"She's better than I am." Georgie said, still not convinced.

"Maybe we're a better team." Dave said, looking at Jason, who nodded encouragement. "Did you hear the guitarist hit the wrong notes?" He shuddered.

"You heard that?!" Jason looked at him, incredulous.

"Well," Dave blushed again, "it didn't sound right to me."
Jason's grin threatened to split his face. "You're right!" He
clapped Dave heartily on the back while Kipper and Georgie
shared a puzzled look.

WHEN THE SAX MAN PLAYS PART 1 MAKING IT
Chapter 11

Kipper rushed through the corridors backstage, avoiding the hazardous cables and wires, searching. Jason beckoned to him urgently, his frown telling Kipper he had cut it fine, timing wise. As the band were announced, cheering went up: Sophie, Anna and Leanne were in the front row, wolf-whistling as Georgie's Guys took their positions onstage.

Georgie allowed herself a grin at them before her face set into a more serious expression. She was perfectly comfortable wearing her soft black leather trousers and the funky emerald satin blouse her friends had chosen for her. Their shopping trip seemed so many months ago, but in reality, only six weeks had elapsed since then.

She took a few calming breaths, smiling when she heard them chanting her name, catching Jason's eye and smiling at him. She looked too at Kipper, who blew her a kiss, and Dave, who winked at her. They were all on an adrenaline high; she was thankful the adrenaline overtook her nerves. Jason had rigged the auto cue screen at the bottom of the stage with her words, just in case. It was such a sweet gesture. She was determined to not need them, but the reassurance alone was enough.

Jason began the rhythm quietly, building up speed and volume; Kipper's piano and Dave's guitar producing the perfect harmony: Georgie began on cue.

Silence filled the room, but soon Georgie saw the crowd were getting into the music, clapping their hands with the rhythm, no doubt down to her friends in the front row, who had started it all off, the gesture adding such an atmosphere. Georgie relaxed as they reached the chorus, swinging her hips and shoulders with the beat.

As the end of the song approached, Georgie took a few steps backwards, finishing the song and gesturing to Jason, then right to Dave, then left to Kipper. Dave lead her to the front of the stage as the crowd roared, making her take a bow, much to her embarrassment and everyone else's amusement.

Cheering and clapping echoed in their ears as the four walked off stage, grinning and congratulating each other.

"We did it!" Georgie was breathless with exhilaration, her eyes shining.

"We've definitely done it!" Kipper boasted. He pointed at Jason, who was looking rather pleased with himself. "You play a mean set of drums for a jazz man."

Jason laughed. "You have to be multi-talented in the music world."

Kipper smiled at him. "I know how we're gonna beat the others, if it comes to it. I've been experimenting; c'mon, come to the set." Kipper lead the way to Music Room 1, their 'set' when the band had a practice session. He slipped into the seat at the piano, indicating for the flushed trio to sit while he played.

Jason's laughter was infectious, though Dave and Georgie didn't know why he was laughing. Kipper's adaptation was wonderful. It had taken the song up a tempo, or perhaps two, Georgie wasn't exactly sure.

"How about me?" Dave queried. "Now my guitar doesn't fit!"

"Yes it does." Kipper spoke patiently. "Just play quicker."

"Quicker?" Dave gulped.

"I'll show you." Jason got up, picking up an electric guitar and plugging it into the nearest amp. He nodded at Kipper, and began to play the adapted version.

Dave nodded, relieved. It was so much easier when he was shown, instead of leaving him to try to imagine, or make his own adaptation.

Georgie's smile disappeared when Kipper suggested she could fit in some sexy dance moves between verses.

"Can't you dance?" He mocked.

"Of course I can dance! I just don't know..." she trailed off.

"What don't you know?" Jason gently probed, not sure what her expression portrayed.

"I don't know if I can dance in public." She allowed herself a small smile as Dave and Kipper laughed. "Laugh all you want, but I don't think I can do it."

"Of course you can." Dave encouraged, smiling at her.

That instant Jason realised Dave fancied Georgie; he might even love her, the way he was looking at her.

Did he do that? His first thought was soon drowned out by the second one. *Did she like Dave?* Jason was sure her attention was pointing in *his* direction, not Dave's but what if he had misinterpreted the signals?

Feeling foolish, he suggested they regrouped again on Monday. He walked away from them, his long strides quickly taking him from the building, leaving the trio behind him confused as to his sudden departure.

"Hey stranger."

The blonde finished her cigarette, grinding out the stub on the pavement before treating him to a full-on beam.

Jason crumbled inwardly. It was the blonde from Fats. Here she was again, sitting on the second step to his flat, waiting for him. He resisted the urge to turn around to see if there was someone behind him; someone else whom she might be referring to. Alas, that was not to be. He groaned, rubbing his head tiredly.

"What's wrong, baby?"

He held one hand up in front of him. "Don't call me that."

"I missed you tonight, sweetie."

Jason pulled another disgusted face.

"Hotty? Cutie?" She tried, taking a few steps towards him.

Jason shook his head. "Get away from me. I don't want you hanging around; you or your brute boyfriend."

"I'm only a concerned friend." She draped herself over him. "Take me upstairs, I'll look after you."

"Get off me!" Jason shook her off. "I... we don't even know each other. What are you doing here?"

WHEN THE SAX MAN PLAYS PART 1 MAKING IT

She pouted, hands on hips. "I was concerned about you. I missed you tonight. Where were you?"

"It doesn't matter," Jason began, immediately cut off.

"It's boring without you, sweet-cheeks, I need to see you." She stood so close, pressing herself against him, Jason was sure he could feel her heartbeat: calm and steady against his racing pulse. Her hands wrapped around his waist, her questing fingers sliding to his hip, fumbling with his belt.

He pushed her off, and though she looked startled, she wasn't dissuaded from her original idea of seducing him - she followed him up a few steps. "Leave me alone." He said, careful to keep his voice level. "I am not interested in you."

"Aww, honey! Don't be like that!"

Jason growled, feeling his annoyance take another step towards insanity, taking another two steps up; still she followed, skipping past him to the top step. He sighed, crossing his arms over his chest, giving her his most serious look. She took a step back, so that she was level with him once more, linking her arm in his, pulling him towards the door.

"Stop harassing me." He pulled away from her, feeling the situation starting to spiral out of his control.

"But sexy, I'm not harassing you." She fluttered her eyelashes, arching her back and thrusting her ample breasts at him. "I'm offering myself to you."

"This is harassment and I'm asking you, very politely, to leave. If you don't, I'll call the police."

"Ooh!" She mocked, rolling her eyes. "I'm sorry to *intrude* on you, sir." She returned to street level.

Jason considered bolting inside and locking the door quick, but images of her on his doorstep, yelling and screaming and banging on the door all night, made him change his mind. His fist closed around the key in his jacket pocket, fighting his conflicting emotions.

She was regarding him warily; like a caged animal waiting to rush the keeper. He didn't trust himself to speak, keeping his expression neutral. In his mind, he was recalling a list of estate agents, part of his brain telling him he was over-exaggerating. While his brain was otherwise engaged, she'd skipped up the steps towards him again. "I'll come back next week, handsome. You'll be ready for me, won't you?" She breathed in his ear. "I won't take no for an answer."

Horror crept into his neutral expression. As she took slow steps away, Jason took equally slow steps back to street level. Reaching the pavement again, he broke into a run as there was a shriek and the sound of high heels clopping after him.

Christopher looked exhausted when he opened the door, his pale face belying his questions. "So you have a stalker now?" He smiled, closing the door behind Jason.

"It's not funny!" Jason crossed the room to the magnificent bay window, casting his unseeing gaze over the landscape. "I hope she doesn't follow me here!"

WHEN THE SAX MAN PLAYS PART 1 MAKING IT

Christopher stopped the quip that had formed on the tip of his tongue, realising his brother was shaking.

"She won't know where you are." He poured a drink, handing over the glass. Jason regarded the honey-coloured liquid for a moment, then downed the concoction without thinking. Christopher took the glass from him to refill it while he choked. "That's 18%, go easy!"

Jason nodded, thinking his throat was on fire.

"What happened? Did she follow you home again?"

Jason shook his head, taking something more than a sip but less than a gulp this time. "Didn't go tonight, it was the audition." Christopher frowned. "You told me Miracle's audition was on Wednesday night?"

Jason realised then that his brother only had half the story... He sighed. To explain it all would take most of the night, he felt sure.

Chapter 12

On Monday morning, Jason breathed a sigh of relief to see that Georgie's Guys had achieved a top ten ranking from their audition. He could tell they were stung that they too hadn't achieved number one; nonetheless, they were easily cajoled - what mattered was qualification, and they had easily achieved this.

Now they would focus on polishing their performance, as Miracle would also. He left them with his congratulations, reminding them of that evening's practice session.

Sitting in Music Room 1, he smiled, feeling a sense of calm. This was the only place he felt safe. The weekend had been hopelessly ruined by that woman... and he didn't even know her. Jason took a deep breath, chiding himself, knowing *he* himself had been his own destruction.

His mind jumped. Of course nothing would happen between him and Georgie. The world was opening up for her, as it was for the rest of the students; on the other hand, he was settling into his established groove.

He winced. Only, now it was time to move.

Uncreasing the daily paper, he flicked through until he found the real estate section. He wasn't interested in the other pages, which was a shame as he missed the interview with Hamish regarding this year's Talent Contest: an article that would have opened his eyes in many ways. His first class was some ninety minutes in the future, so there was plenty time to study the important listings.

He skipped past the large properties, starting from £3.4 million. He snorted: this was more like *unreal* estate, he smiled with the thought.

It looked hopeless, even after twenty minutes' scrutiny. The thought struck him that he was left with renting, so he flicked through the pages again to the relevant section. Again, the search proved fruitless.

He only wanted the basics: somewhere reasonably priced, with good transport links and security. He sighed, wondering if coffee would help: however, the cupboard was bare. Physically he sagged, not sure he could deal with the day without a caffeine boost. A thought crossed his mind: the Union Bar would still be serving breakfast, including coffee. He grabbed his jacket, his wallet therein, closing the door behind him, leaving the paper open on his desk.

That evening, he detected an Atmosphere. Kipper and Dave had arrived together, but Georgie arrived late. Not a problem, Jason reassured her, but he wondered what her reason was, as she had never been late before.

"We should practice the jazzed-up version." He looked at the trio in front of him. "Give us some spice. What do you lot think?" Georgie shrugged, Dave nodded and Kipper grinned.

"What did I say wrong?" Jason said to nobody in particular.

Georgie shook her head and Kipper shrugged.

"Nothing." Dave answered, his expression puzzled.

"Okay." Jason shook his head, wondering if he was imagining it. "We've got quite a bit of work to do. I was thinking of having an extended intro." He looked at Georgie. "Get us into the swing of it, before the first verse."

"You're going to make a mockery of me, are you?" Georgie spoke quietly, looking at Kipper.

Ah... Pieces clicking into place in Jason's mind: it was the dancing that was bothering her.

"Would I do that?" Kipper asked, putting on his innocent expression. It was the same innocent expression he'd worn when he portrayed Jason as a bully at their first meeting; a memory that infuriated her further.

"You bloody would!" Georgie exploded.

Dave and Jason shared a look, wondering what had happened between the feuding pair.

She explained: "If you saw the lurid video he made me watch - he wanted me dirty dancing!"

"It has a different name now." Kipper smirked.

Dave was looking at him, open-mouthed, shaking his head.

Without a word, Jason got up and left the room. Minutes later, he returned with his laptop. "If there'll be any fancy footwork, it'll be of this kind." He said, pressing 'play'.

There was a triumphant glint in Georgie's eyes as the video reeled, and for a moment, Jason wondered if she was going to kiss him, such was her look of gratitude. "That's definitely my style." She agreed, shooting a look at Kipper, daring him to comment.

Another notice was pinned to the Music notice board the following morning, inviting the qualifiers to attend the second round. Again Miracle and Georgie's Guys were separated, one on Thursday 19th, the other on Friday 20th March.

   Jason was surprised there were only two qualification sessions, having calculated for three as there were so many performers. Each session would last four hours: he groaned inwardly; that put paid to his evening flat hunting.

   "Are you sure we don't have to polish up our act?" Michael's worried voice reached Jason's ears.

Jason smiled at him. "Everyone needs to polish up their act. We need to perform to the best of our ability to win."

   "Same time, same place?" Michael smiled back.

Jason nodded. "Put your thinking cap on, I'm looking for ideas."

   "What for?" Michael dropped his voice.

   "I'll tell you all later." Jason replied secretively.

The idea struck Jason as he ate lunch at his desk. Consulting his watch, he knew his brother would be available for a jovial ten minute conversation during his own lunch break.

   "Can you?" Jason's voice was full of relief.

Christopher laughed. "If you're sure you trust me."

"Of course I do! You can also tell me how big the estate agents' lies are." Jason too laughed.

Christopher laughed again. It felt good to laugh. Recently he had dealt his favourite patients a difficult set of cards: breaking it to a new mum that she had three months to live; having to tell one man that there was a chance he would never have kids; but the worst was the six-year-old with leukaemia. It was the part of his job he absolutely *hated*. Of course, it didn't all pan out awfully. There seemed a sort of ying-yang effect in medicine, good mixed with bad as if to balance life. But if anyone knew life was not a balance, it was Christopher.

"Thank you." The gratitude sounded deep in Jason's voice. "Really, you have no idea how this puts me at ease."

"I think it's entirely unnecessary." Christopher began.

Jason sighed. "I just don't want any repercussions."

"Or concussions." Christopher teased, knowing the line could be classed as below the belt, wondering whether his brother would take the joke.

"Or worse." Jason sighed again, neither acknowledging or resenting Christopher's jest.

"Listen here!" The man had lifted Kipper from his chair, holding him aloft by his neck. "You're pulling out of the comp. Go tell your girlfriend." He dropped Kipper back onto the chair, which collapsed under him.

"Piss off!" Kipper spat, springing to his feet.

WHEN THE SAX MAN PLAYS PART 1 MAKING IT

"Watch your mouth!"

Kipper realised the man in front of him was easily 6' 4", weighed eighteen stone plus - and had tattooed knuckles. Another point worth noting was the fact that his huge arms were the width of Kipper's neck. Nonetheless, he never backed down. "We're not pulling out of anything!" Kipper folded his arms in front of him, unaware they were now the centre of attention in the College canteen.

Dave had been a few steps behind the man who'd approached Kipper, stopping when he heard the conversation. He was now taking small, slow steps in the opposite direction. If he had been in his position, he'd keep quiet, but he knew Kipper wouldn't think. Jason was right, Kipper *never* engaged his brain before opening his mouth.

In the safety of the doorway, Dave first considered his actions cowardly, but when a full blown fight ensued, he congratulated himself for trusting his intuition. His feet were rooted to the spot, as was his gaze as the table broke when Kipper landed across it, scattering chairs and students to the four corners of the hall. Then the man leant over Kipper, grabbing his shirt in his fist to lift him from the floor. "I won't have you interfering with my girlfriend's dream!" He roared, before dropping him again.

Dave flattened himself against the wall as the man stalked out. As if time had stopped and then started up again, everyone moved at once. Some people carried on eating their lunch and talking amongst themselves; some went over to the debris and

Kipper. Again, instinct kicked in: Dave re-entered the room, heading to his friend's side.

"It was kind of him to not break your fingers." He joked as Kipper stood up and brushed himself down.

Kipper laughed, despite his protesting bruises, nursing his sore knuckles from where he'd dealt the first punch.

"WHAT IS GOING ON HERE?" Hamish bellowed, striding across the room, surveying the damage, his gaze landing on Kipper. He pointed a finger at him. "I might have known it would be *you*! Explain yourself!"

For once in his life, Kipper stuttered and ran out of steam.

"It wasn't his fault." Dave piped up in his defence.

"I'll see both of you in my office, in five minutes." Hamish turned on his heel, leaving them to regroup. "BE THERE!"

Dave shuddered.

Chapter 13

Jason put his head in his hands, unable to believe what the last 48 hours had produced for him, reflecting that it was a typical Friday the 13th. They were due a practice session tonight, with the second qualification rounds looming, but he wasn't sure how it was going to go ahead.

Dave and Georgie were extremely nervous after the incident on Wednesday, two days ago now; Kipper's bruises were keeping him quiet; and to top things off, Christopher had phoned not long ago to say that the blonde was again sitting on the steps to his flat. He'd had the police remove her, but that wasn't enough in Jason's mind. He knew his brother thought him crazy to want to move, but at least now Christopher knew it was not a fabrication of his addled mind. He really did not relish the idea of practice. Sacrifice was one thing, but in this state, would it do any of them any good?

"Can't we regroup on Monday?" Georgie suggested.

Jason sighed, thinking that Monday would be no better.

"Surely a weekend of rest would be a good idea?" She continued, resting her hand lightly on his shoulder.

Silently she was cursing the way he was always so quiet; so distant. They all knew something was wrong, knowing it wasn't just the trouble with the band and the jealous unknown rival.

"Jason?" She squeezed his shoulder, bringing him from his trance.

"Sorry." He looked up at her, his expression pained.

"Cancel tonight. We can't work like this." She squeezed his shoulder again, surprised when he put his hand on top of hers.

"No, it's fine." He gave her a half-smile. "Unless you think it'd be best? Kipper must be in pain: it's brave of him to continue."
But typical of his stubborn nature. his brain continued. He smiled to himself.

"Let me talk to them." Georgie said softly.

Jason nodded, sinking back into his gloom. If they found out who was behind the attack, the group would be banned, the students would be expelled. Hamish wanted to expel Kipper, until he discovered the truth in his story, with CCTV footage providing adequate proof on Kipper's behalf.

When Jason had returned to the Music block the next day after lunch, he found Hamish pacing outside his section. Diving headlong into the first room, Jason had stopped when he saw the room had been trashed. Two other rooms were the same: desks and chairs smashed; equipment ruined; paperwork burning in the bins. Furious ranting had exploded through him before he could stop it; as the fire alarm sounded, the automatic sprinkler system activated.

Now, a day later, his section looked almost normal. Fortunately the double lock on the instrument room hadn't been broken, enabling classes to continue. Different chairs and tables had been drafted in, meaning they were still able to function. Jason sighed again.

Georgie put her head round the door once more, seeing Jason hadn't moved in the last hour. She pulled up a chair beside him. "It wasn't personal." She said softly, trying to meet his gaze. He laughed harshly. "It feels like it."

"I know." She paused. "The guys aren't sure, maybe it'd do us good to have a break?"

"We can't let them beat us." Jason spoke suddenly, turning a fiery glare on her.

"We're not." She unravelled one of his clenched fists, taking it in hers. "We're just regrouping. There's nothing wrong in that. We have Kipper as our excuse."

Jason nodded, her comfort was thawing the ice surrounding him, he realised. He smiled at her, squeezing her hand, not wanting to let go, just yet. "Okay. I'll pander to your whims, just this once." She smiled at him; silence fell between them.

"I'm glad you weren't here." She said quietly, moments later.

"They wouldn't have *dared* if I had been." His reply shot back. Georgie shook her head. "I think you're wrong - they sought out Kipper. God knows what they would've done to you." She shuddered, remembering the snapped necks of the guitars.

Jason looked up at her, seeing her concern in her eyes, his heart skipping a beat. Seconds passed as he fell speechless, knowing that this was an ideal time to reassure her; even to kiss her, if that was what they both wanted. But did she? He was overrun with emotion. To think that this beautiful woman *cared* about him... He jolted from his thoughts as her lips pressed against his.

The kiss lasted all of three seconds. Georgie pulled away from him, scraping back her chair and leaping to her feet, murmuring her apology.

Jason caught up with her at the door, resting his hand on hers, still on the door handle, closing it again. Wordlessly he took her face in his hands and kissed her back, relieved to find her respond. He was more than a little taken aback when her tongue found its way into his mouth, teasing him. She pressed herself close to him, sighing happily when he dropped his arms around her waist, leaning her cheek against his shoulder. She squeezed him, her arms secured around his back.

"Georgie..."

"Sshh!" She smiled, pulling away to look into his face. "I know what you're going to say. We can't do this, not while we're student and teacher. But when I graduate..." Her voice, usually so bubbly and full of confidence, faltered.

"Of course." He hugged her in close, the grin threatening to split his face. He sighed. "Until then, we need to act normal." He was thankful that she was so sensible and forward-thinking; thankful also that she could read his mind.

Georgie blushed. "Will you court me properly?"

"If you like." Jason laughed. "But you may have to guide me. Candlelit dinners; champagne picnics in the park; nights in with your favourite takeaway and a great DVD. Even a meal with your parents, I'm not frightened of the in-laws."

Georgie winced. "Perhaps you'll change your mind when you actually meet them."

Jason sighed, squeezing her. "They can't be worse than mine." She hated hearing the pain enter his voice, distracted from her thoughts when he ever so gently kissed her nose.

She giggled. "Our secret for a few months?"

Jason nodded, smiling; aware of the relief coursing through his veins.

Chapter 14

I'D LIKE TO SEE UR FLAT, WHERE DO U LIVE? XXX

Georgie loved the idea of a secret rendezvous at his flat. That was another problem with living with her parents, she couldn't invite him round whenever she wanted.

IN MIDST OF MOVING, SORRY XXX

Georgie's heart leapt at the thought of him leaving London.

NOT TOO FAR I HOPE? WANT YOU NEARBY! XXX

She chewed her lip, reviewing the message before sending it.

WHEREVER I CAN AFFORD. HOPELESS SEARCH. XXX

Georgie knew the feeling well. She pulled a sympathetic face, compiling her reply.

I KNOW PEOPLE IN PROPERTY. I CAN HELP. XXX

Jason smiled reading her reply. What harm would it do to have her help? Nothing he found in his rental range was suitable.

WHEN THE SAX MAN PLAYS PART 1 MAKING IT

OK. 2-BED; GD TRNSPRT LINKS; SECURITY ENTRY; £975 P/M. THANKS. XXX

Georgie nodded to herself, firing up her laptop. After ten minutes she had an e-mail ready to go, adding "Decent Area Only", sure that this was a silent requirement.

"You look different." Her father accused, waving his porridge spoon across the table at her the next morning.

Georgie's eyebrows shot up. Since when did he take any notice of how she looked?

"I hope you've not changed your mind about MacMillan's?"

"No!" Georgie hated how he regarded her over his glasses as if she wasn't important. "I can't wait for May." She blushed, mentally adding *for many reasons.* There was their holiday, her new job - and Jason. She sighed dreamily.

It was enough for her father, who returned to his paper and his porridge. After breakfast, Georgie went to her room to collect her bag and books for the day ahead. She caught her reflection in the mirror, scrutinising her appearance. Did she look different? She'd never been in love before, but apparently those under the spell of love glowed. Was she glowing?

A thought struck her - their girlie holiday would be at the start of her relationship with Jason. What if something happened while she was away? What if he met someone else? What if *she* met someone else? Two weeks could be a long time, in the wrong circumstances.

Georgie shook herself, certain that she wouldn't find anyone quite like Jason and certain also - in the special way that love gives confidence - that he would not be looking, whether she was in the country or not. She made her way to Impervious that morning, beaming at the world around her. Sophie was the first on her train, and immediately latched onto her happiness - detecting the infamous glow no doubt, Georgie thought wryly.

Kipper tried to focus on the ceiling swirling above him, constant bleeping from the alarm telling him to get up. He groaned. Monday mornings were the worst; worse still if you'd been beaten up the previous week. He was sure he should be recovering by now... the thought made his overactive imagination run wild. The horror of his train of thought made him sit up. His destiny was in his hands and it would take more than one man to upset him. He would succeed if it killed him!

The week passed in a flash. Soon, it was Thursday's audition and Jason sat with Miracle in the wings, watching the other performers, voicing the fact that they should be aware everyone was competition.
Kipper laughed, wincing as his battered ribs throbbed.
"But it's true!" Michael agreed. "We're all against each other. That's what the competition is about."
Kipper rolled his eyes. "I know *that*!" He tutted. "But they're

nothing compared to us. Technically they *are* our competition, but we're gonna win hands down!"

Jason laughed then. "I love your confidence."

"I wish you'd give me some." Dave shuddered, feeling sick.

Kipper rolled his eyes again. "When are we were on?"

"Second from now."

"But we don't have to stay all night?" He continued.

"Not if you don't want to." Jason smiled to himself, knowing Georgie was in the audience to support them. He would be staying; sitting with her. It all looked above board, and harmless. "I'm staying, as there may be clues to glean from watching - plus I may find some new recruits for next year."

"I want to join you next year." Michael's voice took on a hint of bravado.

Jason snapped from his thoughts. "You want a career in Music?"

Michael blushed, but Jason didn't give him a chance to speak. "You need a professional voice coach, there's only so much a lowly Music tutor can do." He smiled at him, thankful the youngster hadn't properly thought out the idea.

"But you'll help me?" Michael's voice took on a pleading tone.

Jason nodded. "Of course."

"Thanks." Michael's blush deepened, trying to hide his disappointment, knowing that what Jason had said was true.

Jason strode away from the group, uncasing his trusty sax, sighing contentedly as his hands fell into the same grooves on the instrument's body. He had plans to explore his lover's body; to know it blindfold, as he knew his trusty old friend. His other instrument would appreciate that... he wondered if his unusual twist of thought could be considered crass. He almost laughed aloud, stopping, sure that the rest of the group would not share the joke.

Another thought crossed his mind: he was convinced Dave's affections lay with Georgie. He couldn't blame Dave, love worked in mysterious ways after all, but it was horrible to fall into unrequited love. *It was unrequited love, wasn't it?* The very thought made him frown.

Fortunately, his thoughts were interrupted before they ran away with him: Miracle were called. He took several deep breaths, taking in the backstage bustle around them. His trademark grin settled across his face as he lead the group out onto the stage.

An expectant hush fell over the audience, clapping politely as the performers found their places. The lights came up as Vince began to drum, the rhythm increasing as the intro played out. Kipper and Dave played flawlessly, and Michael began on cue this time: then and only then, Jason felt himself relax.

The best part of performing was knowing your music inside out, thus allowing yourself to go with the flow, safe in the knowledge that everything sounded terrific. Having an appreciative audience also helped. It was strange to play in Impervious' main hall, as the lighting meant you could see everyone in the crowd: usually performers could see only the first few rows as the rest of the auditorium was in darkness. It was a

WHEN THE SAX MAN PLAYS PART 1 MAKING IT

completely different experience, Jason reflected. He wondered if Miracle could make it in the real music world; becoming truly famous; touring Britain before conquering Europe...

He realised his ultimate dream likely would never, realistically, come true. But that was what dreams were for ...for dreaming.

He bowed to the crowd's rapturous applause as they finished, leading his co-musicians offstage, enjoying their excited expressions, sure that their adrenaline was still pumping, as his was. Performing gave him such an indescribable thrill; he loved the idea of entertaining thousands with his music, which made the dream all the more real.

"If we win," Michael began.

"When." Kipper interrupted, smiling at him.

"When we win," Michael began again, "could we be good enough to go pro?"

Jason laughed, taking several minutes to answer the question. He could see they were all waiting for his reply. "I don't know, but it doesn't do any harm to dream. All we can do is perform to the best of our abilities." He grinned at Kipper. "Having reviewed the competition so far, I'd say it's a safe bet we have a place in the Quarterfinals, but perhaps I shouldn't tempt Fate."

Kipper grinned back. "I'd say you're right."

The following night Kipper and Dave were visibly buoyed by the fact that Miracle had won a place in the Quarterfinals. Georgie was excited for them, but secretly burned with jealousy, unsure how she would cope if they didn't get through tonight. She was still worried about their main rivals, The Polars (an apt name as they thought they were so cool, Kipper snorted when he heard the story behind the name), especially as they had her song - and worse still, they were on first. Georgie prayed that they wouldn't be called immediately afterwards, but the playlist dictated thus.

"She's got nothing on you." Kipper's voice broke through her worried thoughts. "Don't worry, we're cruising through." He dropped his arm around her shoulders, talking quietly to her, squeezing her, his mouth centimetres from her ear.

Jason felt the fizz of jealousy rip through him. He forced himself to take deep breaths, reminding himself that Kipper was just being Kipper and he wasn't intending to do anything to her.

He glanced at Dave, who's green-eyed monster was stamped across his face. *Ah...* The confirmation of Jason's thoughts gave him neither solace nor triumph. He walked over, trying to get him focused on the challenge once more. Dave agreed to a one-to-one session later with a nod of his heavy head, seeing Jason's understanding reflected in his gaze. He knew then he was safe to confide in Jason; the strong, sensible one of the group: he was the perfect confidante. He smiled when Jason put his arm around his shoulders, nodding his readiness.

A few 'boos' rang out as Georgie's Guys with "Say What You Want" were announced: Georgie's positivity dived to her boots.

"We'll show them!" Jason shouted indignantly, as much for the reassurance of the trio in front of him as the crowd. "Play like you have never played before and everything will be fine."

Kipper nodded. "Yeah! Fuck them! We're the best!"

Georgie and Dave grinned at each other, seeing Jason was trying not to laugh. Seconds later, Jason counted them in before softly beginning to drum. Kipper began simultaneously, the electronic keyboard being played to full effect. Mid week, they had favoured the keyboard over piano, Kipper arguing it matched their jazzed-up tune better. Jason admitted defeat, hoping Kipper wouldn't get used to having his own way!

Jason hit the drums a little harder, a little faster, his brain already pounding out the rhythm in his head, aware he had to steady himself or he would ruin the whole act. By now, Dave had joined in, his expression mixed with fear and concentration.

The second he'd agreed to switch to an electric guitar last week, Jason had swung an amp at his feet and plugged him in. Poor Dave had nearly keeled over there and then, totally overwhelmed. There weren't many differences: only the feel of the guitar, the sound and weight - but the fundamentals were the same. He had taken a lot of convincing, and more than once, Jason wished Kipper would sling some of his bucket loads of confidence over his nervous friend.

Risking a glance across at the rest of the band Jason took in the performers mid-flow. Georgie was putting heart and soul into the music. Kipper too was giving the piece *hell* and it sounded fabulous. He might be a pain to work with, but Jason realised then that he had more talent than he'd been given credit for.

WHEN THE SAX MAN PLAYS PART 1 MAKING IT

A place in the Quarterfinals would assure Dave that they were forerunners in the competition, giving his self-esteem a well deserved boost - everyone would feel the same with a win. Was there an edge of a smile on Dave's face? Jason thought it was the light playing tricks, but maybe not.

He began to wind down, hitting the last part of the song. He saw Georgie indicate to some unknown in the crowd, as if her whole performance had been for her lover in the crowd. How ironic that her true lover was behind, and not in front of, her.

Jason allowed one pause more than last time to absorb the atmosphere before heading offstage, sure that they were all following behind him. A loud whistle attracted his attention: Kipper was gesturing for him to come back. Jason frowned, wondering what was going on, but nevertheless headed back out onto the stage, blushing furiously as the crowd applauded him. He raised his hands in a thank-you gesture, applauding the crowd and side-stepping into the safety of the wings, watching his amused band mates take their time.

He shook his head, laughing. He'd spotted Hamish and the evaluating judges: Hamish treated him to a thumbs-up. That was a vote of confidence if ever he'd seen one!

Chapter 15

Miracle shared number one with another band! Vince realised his first feeling was of disappointment. He hadn't realised until then what winning meant to him, and the fact it didn't matter what position they achieved escaped his brain.

"Oh.My.God!" Michael jumped up and down, barely unable to contain his excitement.

Kipper approached the notice board, which by now was nearly obscured by highly-strung students, all jostling to see which position they had achieved, dreading being last and ultimately dropped. Amazingly, the crowd parted to let him in, where Vince and Michael had fought to be five minutes previously.

"Well done!" Someone called from the crowd behind them. Kipper turned around, nodding and smiling, raising his finger in the air, proclaiming he was number one. Some people laughed, some walked off disgusted.

Vince and Michael were shocked to see Georgie's Guys had made a dramatic leap up the rankings to claim fifth place overall. But, better still, they had ousted The Polars!

Jason sighed, running his hands through his short flame-red hair. His pale face was crinkled with anxiety as he looked around the table. He'd called the two groups to a meeting in the Union Bar, wanting to cancel their next practice.

"You said you can never practice too much." Vince pointed out.

"Are you losing confidence in us?" Dave hardly dared breathe the suggestion, meeting Jason's eyes and looking away again, fearing the answer was going to be 'yes'.

"No, of course not." He took a deep breath. "I didn't want to upset anyone, I just feel that we can practice less. We don't need constant drill."

"I thought," Kipper began and Jason rolled his eyes, knowing whatever was coming was going to be derogatory. "You said every time we practice we'll get better, so surely at this stage we should be practising more?"

"You mean you don't feel you've already given your best?" An angry tone crept into Jason's voice.

Kipper shrugged. "I'm just repeating what you said."

"We don't need a parrot." Jason snapped. "Let's take a vote: We have Tuesday, Thursday and the weekend off - all in favour raise your hand."

Vince's hand was first, followed by Michael. Georgie too raised her hand, smiling at Jason.

Dave was anxiously looking at Kipper. "I think it's a good idea." He said after a while. "After all, we don't want burnout. It's okay for us, we're doing two songs, but aren't you two fed up doing the same thing?" He looked at Vince and Michael, waiting while they nodded. "And aren't you fed up getting home late every night?" He turned to Jason.

Jason shrugged. "I haven't got anything to keep me busy." He pulled a face. "Apart from flat hunting."

"Flat hunting?" Vince echoed.

"You don't want to talk about me. Drink anyone?"

Minutes later, he placed the drinks tray carefully on the table, correctly placing each glass in front of the corresponding drinker.

"What's wrong the place you have now?" Georgie asked. She was aware that she couldn't let on what she knew, but also that she didn't know every detail, or even many details... Jason was very secretive.

Jason sighed. "Nothing." He traced the condensation on the outside of his glass.

"You don't sound like a man who wants to move, so what's happening?" Kipper began, taking a mouthful of his beer, aware that there was something Jason wasn't saying.

"I feel I have to."

"And?" Kipper prompted.

"And." Jason paused, taking a deep breath. "I need to for my sanity." He gave them a wry smile. "I have a stalker."

"Good God!" Vince put his glass down, shocked.

"A stalker?" Michael repeated, wondering if he'd been seen in the shadows at Fats. "Are you sure?"

Jason nodded. "Remember last month's black eye?" He paused until they all nodded. "My stalker's boyfriend."

There was a moment of silence while the five contemplated this.

"Your stalker's a woman?" Georgie half-laughed.

"I wish it was funny." Jason pulled a face.

"I don't mean it like that." Georgie flustered. "I mean... do you know her?" She ignored the relief flooding Michael's face, second-guessing what was going through his mind, having heard the same rumours Jason had.

Jason shook his head. "She's a fellow performer at Fats. She latched onto me after the first time I played a Friday night; she jumped into my cab, I couldn't get rid of her." He realised then how pathetic it all sounded. "She won't leave me alone."

"She's seducing you?" Kipper grinned. "Is she good looking?"

"Shut up!" Dave punched Kipper's arm. "That's not funny. You don't know nowadays. She could have a knife, a gun; anything." Jason's face whitened, having not had that thought before.

"I'm sure she's not like that." Georgie jumped in. "She's probably just off her head."

Jason looked at her. "Off her head to fancy me?" He watched Georgie's expression change several times: sympathy-shock-embarrassment. Then he laughed. "I reckon you're right. It's the beefcake boyfriend that worries me."

Vince frowned. "Where does her boyfriend come in?"

"He follows her. He grabbed her the first time, punching me." Michael's eyes widened. "This has happened more than once?"

"Weekly." Jason closed his eyes. "Last week I didn't go home, I went to my brother's in Kensington."

Kipper gave a low appreciative whistle at the mention of the prestigious address, cut short by Dave's nudge.

"Christopher didn't believe me, so he went round to see for himself. Ended up getting the police involved." Jason leant back in his chair, blowing out a deep sigh. "Hence the flat hunting."

"What're you going to do - a midnight flit?" Kipper joked.

Jason laughed. "I'm considering it. I want to have a place to rent before I put it on the market. It might take ages to sell up."

Figures clicked into Georgie's mind. She *had* thought his rental figure was low, although she had no idea what his income was.

"Guys, no sympathy please." Jason realised they were all looking at him in exactly that light. "I'm fine."

"Until the beefcake catches up with you again." Michael voiced the thought before he could stop it.

Jason shuddered. "Exactly what I want to avoid." He sighed, consulting his watch. "She'll be sitting waiting for me now."

"You can't sneak past?" Kipper asked.

"Why should he sneak into his own place?" Dave answered.

"I couldn't." Jason shook his head. "Even if I could, who's to say she wouldn't still be there the next morning?"

"No!" Michael and Georgie gasped.

Jason shook his head. "Nope, not worth it." He laughed gently. "It's starting to play on my nerves now." He admitted. "But I have my escape plan." He shrugged. "So if we're in agreement to cut Tuesday, Thursday and the weekend?" He looked around the table, smiling at their eager nods. "Just until the next stage." He paused for dramatic effect, seeing confusion in their expressions. "Should we make the Final, we need to have another song prepared."

As they collectively gasped, his wide smile returned.

Chapter 16

"Another song?" Dave greeted him the following morning, sitting in the same place, prearranged as of ten minutes ago.

This was becoming the Music booth, Jason smiled to himself. Every time one of them wanted to talk, he suggested the Union Bar, and they sat in one of the back booths, ensuring peace.

Smithy gave him a nod any time he entered or exited; Jason always nodded back out of politeness, unable to read the bar manager's expression. One experienced a lot working behind a bar: Jason guessed that Smithy knew all of Impervious' gossip, carefully storing the thought, planning to exploit it sometime in the future.

He flashed Dave a sympathetic smile. "Perhaps I should have told you before everyone else, but I knew you'd be fine."

"*How the hell can I be FINE*?!" Horror filled Dave's face. "It's bad enough as it is trying to play the right song without giving me ANOTHER!"

"You *will* be fine." Jason spoke earnestly, believing everything would turn out perfectly. "I probably shouldn't say this, but I'm sure one of us will win, and I'm pretty sure I know which one."

"You're going to say Miracle, aren't you?" Shocked, Dave's jaw dropped open when Jason shook his head. "WHAT?!"

Jason chuckled. "Keep your voice down." He looked around, ensuring nobody was near enough to eavesdrop.

Dave was still incredulous. "You can't be serious!"

Jason kept quiet, letting the information sink in.

"What do you know?" Dave's eyes narrowed.

Jason laughed. "There's no need to be suspicious! I don't *know* anything! It's performance evaluation - Georgie's Guys rate better than Miracle."

Dave raised one eyebrow, willing him to continue.

"The song has an upbeat tempo that will get the votes, it's well known, and crucially, we have female sex appeal. The Final is decided by the judges but the students' vote is also counted on to find an overall winner - and Impervious has more male than female students. The guys aren't going to vote Michael over Georgie." Jason laughed, tickled by that scenario.

"They might." Dave started, suddenly feeling defensive.

Jason's smile became serious. "But this isn't set in stone; it's not guaranteed. Let's just keep this between us."

They both jumped as Smithy's shadow fell over them.

"That's fascinating." He beamed at the two men in front of him, receiving two horrified looks before disappearing back towards the bar, still talking, his bluetooth earpiece flashing.

Jason's sigh of relief had them both laughing.

That evening's practice was full of high spirits. Jason hoped it wouldn't turn ugly between the two groups should one of them not make the next round. While he was certain he was tutoring two finalists, he did not truly know what would happen.

He had made recordings of the groups, and was planning a

'listening', unsure of what they would make of this idea. Nonetheless he put his fears to one side, as he often did. There was an instinct deep inside of him that led him successfully in times like this, 'turbulence in his confidence' was his own phrase.

"This is going to sound daft, so I've cut it down to choruses. I want us all to listen; see if we can learn what distinguishes a good performance and a great performance."

"You mean like bum notes?" Kipper teased.

Jason nodded, trying not to take the bait. "Yes, but generally what sounds professional and what sounds rough. You'll see what I mean." He gave them all a sheet of paper, with the numbers 1 to 10 written down one side. "Write your comments if you want, see if we agree. There's no right or wrong," he added, seeing Dave's panic-stricken look. "But I'm sure you all know what sounds right." He was pleased to receive several nods, proceeding to play the recordings.

Dave drew him to one side as the rest filed past them an hour later. His blank expression meant Jason couldn't guess what was going through his mind. "I see what you mean, about the bands." Jason nodded, waiting to see if he would comment further.

"I think you're right." He grinned at him. "Even if you aren't, I've got a bloody good chance of being in the Final, haven't I?" Jason laughed. "Are you getting used to your taste of fame?" He teased.

Dave too laughed.

WHEN THE SAX MAN PLAYS PART 1 MAKING IT

The following night, Jason hovered by the flat's entrance, his collar folded up against the stiff breeze, wishing he had a car to wait for the estate agent in. It would be warm and safe, Jason caught himself thinking, his eyes darting around the street. Was this a reputable area? He didn't like the look of the gang of smoking youths congregated by the nearest lamppost, not ten yards away. Although he was reasonably self-assured, there was something unsafe about the eight to one situation that *could* erupt here.

Jason shuddered, and at that second, a car screeched to a halt beside him. To his relief, it was the estate agent - Paul someone, Jason hadn't managed to catch his surname, as they insisted on being 'modern' and calling everyone by their first names in the office. Clients, however, were still politely referred to by their surname.

"Mr Bottelli, my apologies for keeping you waiting." Paul simultaneously jumped out of his car, crushed out his fag end and bounded towards him, pumping his hand vigourously. "Welcome to 12 St Germain's Close, your new bachelor pad." He nudged Jason's arm in a conniving manner. "I bet you can't wait to get inside, eh?" He gave Jason a knowing wink, throwing his arm around Jason's shoulders, guiding him up the steps.

"Actually, yes." Jason replied, unable to take his eyes off the youths.

He regretted the decision to view this place the second they entered. The hallway was littered with plasterboard; a glance upwards revealed it was ceiling plasterboard. Scenes of devastation followed: the walls throughout the tiny flat were full of holes and the wooden floors were riddled with woodworm. The kitchen unit doors were hanging off, and the linoleum floor was cracked and split. By then, Jason had seen enough.

Paul saw his appalled expression. "Ready when you are." His voice shrunk to a dispirited level, following Jason out.

Jason took several deep breaths back outside in the chilly, damp air, thankful at least that it was relatively clean - they were in London after all.

"Anyway!" Paul spoke brightly, again slinging his arm around Jason's shoulders. "I'm sure the next place will be better."

"Can't be worse, can it?" Jason looked at him, risking a small smile: Paul did not return the smile. *What other horrors has he got in store for me?* Jason wondered; little time for thought as he climbed into Paul's litter-strewn car and hung on for his life as the estate agent drove like a maniac to their next destination.

Forty minutes and two flats later, Jason's phone bleeped a message from Georgie. Glad of the distraction, he clicked 'open', seeing that she was recommending another estate agent to him, Graham. Heaving a sigh of relief, he excusing himself to make the call in peace.

Graham was a laid-back rental agent who sympathised with his plight, reassuring him that he would guide him through the horrors that were out there. Jason laughed then, telling him he was viewing such horrors right now! Graham asked him to come to his office so that they could discuss his requirements in full and Jason gladly obliged, cutting short his evening of viewings with Paul.

Graham had two mugs of steaming freshly-ground coffee on his desk when Jason arrived, bedraggled from the Spring evening rain. He dismissed Jason's apologies for dripping rainwater over his office, beckoning him to be seated, offering milk and sugar to Jason's taste.

Over the next thirty minutes Jason's sorry tale unwound; he saw Graham nodding understandingly every time he looked up. Jason was then presented with a folder of what Graham thought were suitable apartments. Taking his time flipping through the selection, he was impressed that Graham called up on his laptop the viewing papers on those he expressed an interest in straight away.

Graham's expression turned to mischief once business was over, and the appointments were made to Jason's schedule. He hadn't failed to notice that the mention of Georgie's name sent a flush to his new client's cheeks...

Chapter 17

Jason sat in the Union Bar, sipping his espresso whilst reviewing Graham's printouts from the previous evening. Appointments to visit the four apartments he was interested in were split over the rest of the week; Graham had offered to pick him up on Thursday evening, a kind offer that Jason refused. He hated feeling he was putting people out; worse still was asking favours. It helped when people were so obliging - like Georgie offering to help him flat hunt and pointing him in Graham's direction.

He knew that Georgie's offer had been warm and sincere, whereas Graham - nice though he was - was only in it for the commission: Jason didn't hold this against him, knowing it was purely business. He had been surprised last night when Graham had enquired what his relationship was with Georgie. Had his blush given him away? Jason frowned at that thought, hoping that nobody at Impervious would connect the pair, unsure of how, and indeed if, he could swerve the conversation.

Georgie too was thinking about their relationship. Her tutors had agreed on final examination dates, and for those who felt ready, the first sitting could be arranged for a weeks' time.

Her parents, once privy to this information, agreed that it would be best for her to attend the first sitting. MacMillan's had offered her a position based on the prediction that she would achieve a top grade, and having interviewed her, felt sure that she would blossom to a considerable asset for the firm within twelve to eighteen months of her in-house training. It was a heavy expectation and the sooner Georgie's results were available, the sooner the pressure would be lifted.

For the first time in her life, Georgie's eyes had been opened to her parents' lifestyle. As well as managing their own careers, they were also managing hers, though it had barely begun. This frightened her.

It wasn't the fact that this was the dog-eat-dog world of Law; nor that she was stepping to a world where the attitude was work hard, play harder. It was more that she would be managed by her parents for the foreseeable future: she was *never* going to step out of their shadow. She had studying through University as they had wanted; she had worked her holidays with both - in turn - of her parents' Law firms, fighting for their approval.

Standing here, watching her parents bustle back and forth, packing up briefcases, laptops and papers, she could literally see the stress weighing them down. On their shoulders was the weight of expectation, day-in, day out. Georgie could see it now, etched into the fine lines on her parents' faces; her mother's especially.

She was struck with the fear that she didn't want to be like that. Trembling with the realisation, she gathered her bag and books for the day, wandering out of the house in a daze, automatically drifting to the Tube station. She was still lost in her thoughts when Sophie sat beside her, yawning and protesting how on Earth you were meant to study for five hours *and* get a decent night's sleep?

Georgie shook her head, trying to get back into normality but also in reply to Sophie's usual morning moans. All she could do was go with the flow, and apply for the first sitting once the class had emptied out that morning. A smile crept over her face: early graduation would mean she was free to pursue a legitimate relationship with Jason sooner than they'd originally thought!

That notion, coupled with her special hot chocolate, set her up for a busy day, aware that the band's practice session tonight meant she wouldn't arrive home until almost nine o'clock. Not that she minded. Her parents always talked 'shop', making conversation very boring in their house. The girls were too polite to tell her that, but Georgie knew it was the truth. And to think that once upon a time she had thought their courtroom tales eccentric and interesting...!

Georgie daydreamed her way through lunch. Unusually she was alone, her three friends occupied with late lectures; nonetheless, she was determined to spend the time purposefully; determined also not to weep over her change of heart concerning her career.

She dived into the book she'd started in September, stopping at the third chapter a week into the term, and carrying it around ever since, wondering if she'd get the chance to finish it. It was a rom-com, Anna had suggested it to her as a bit of light-hearted relief.

WHEN THE SAX MAN PLAYS PART 1 MAKING IT

Georgie's eyes nearly popped out of her head when the steamy sex scene unrolled. She marvelled at how vivid the writing was - it was almost as if the scene was played out in front of her - and she was ashamed to find she felt rather jealous of the heroine. Also, she was rather turned on by the details - the caresses, kisses, nibbles - and soon began to replace the hero's name with Jason's and the heroine's likewise with her own.

Giggling with her thoughts, she was aware that a few students sitting around her had turned their attention to her. The notion struck her that it would be entertaining to write a story of her own. Thus inspired, she began to scribble in her notebook.

The final stage play of the semester was announced and again Kipper landed the lead role. His girlfriend of five weeks, Maya Keene, was given a secondary role - instead, the role for his female sidekick was given to Ericka Meander, a slim brunette with a posh accent and a notorious party-girl attitude.

Kipper's eyes lit up, while Maya's heart sank knowing full well where Kipper's attentions would be drawn. She confronted him with her theory, and he replied that he had to 'feel the part, play the character' and if that meant getting close to Ericka, then that's what he had to do. Maya shook her head despondently, knowing she had already lost him.

"Is Jason The One?" Anna's voice made Georgie jump out of her skin. She smiled her apology, sitting down beside her.

Georgie shrugged, turning her gaze to her friend. "How do you know?"

"You just do." Anna's smile widened to a grin. "I think he's nice. In fact, he's perfect for you."

Georgie smiled, nodding along with her friend's words. "I know he's not the most handsome man in the world."

"Don't you think so?" Anna frowned.

"*I* do, yes. He's perfect in my eyes, but all men have flaws." Anna laughed. "And how do *you* know that?" Her tone insinuated that Georgie's lack of experience would mean she was clueless in this area.

"All you have to do to know that is to listen to other women talking about their men." Georgie too laughed. "Even the ones you thought were perfect."

"Yes, but nobody is truly perfect, we're all human Georgie." She patted Georgie's arm fondly, repeating her first question. "Do you think he's The One?" She lowered her voice.

Georgie blushed, knowing what Anna was getting at. She sighed. "I hope so."

That evening Georgie paid Jason more attention, taking in all the details about him: the way he waved his hands around when he spoke passionately about something; the glint in his eye when he talked about the competition; the expression of happiness that crossed his face when she walked in the room. It all made her smile even wider. He was always smartly dressed, his shoes always polished, his clothes always co-ordinated - and better still, every outfit matched his gorgeous flame-red hair perfectly. She didn't know how he made it look so effortless, but he did.

The following night another message arrived to his phone.

WE NEED TO TALK - MEET ME PLS. G XXX

Jason wondered what the urgency behind this latest text from Georgie was. Hastily he re-pocketed his phone, seeing Graham hurrying up the street towards him, keys already in his hand.

Band practice had gone extremely well the previous night and no-one had shown any nerves; this was unusual considering it was a week until the Quarterfinals. Jason knew at any minute one of his 'students' - and he used the term loosely when describing the band members - may need his reassurance.

"Are you ready?" Graham greeted him.

Jason nodded, knowing he could send Georgie a reply when he was left alone in the flat for a moment's privacy. While he was guided up the stairs, his brain whirled for somewhere they could meet.

He was astounded when Graham ushered him into a newly decorated hallway, shutting the door firmly behind them and locating the light switch. He had apologised for the pile of mail lying on the doormat, which Jason had nearly slid over on, ill-prepared for a slippery reception.

WHEN THE SAX MAN PLAYS PART 1 MAKING IT

Jason had a good feeling about this apartment already, despite almost being knocked off his feet the second he was inside. The whole place was in good order, freshly decorated but small. 'Half-furnished' was a slight understatement: he pondered the bed, table, telephone and washing machine. The view was of Hammersmith railway line: not ideal but not offensive.

Jason took note of the triple-glazing, and just to prove the point a train rattled past, it's progress barely audible. He surveyed the carpeted bedroom - empty except for a bed - and the spare room - empty with bare floorboards - finding them clean and of decent size. Graham told him that it was a long let, and was ready for immediate occupation.

Jason locked eyes with him. Both men knew this was the perfect property - within his specified price; ready for immediate occupation; with good transport links and local amenities not ten minutes' walk from the front door. Situated on the first floor, Jason would have the best view, as well as the luxury of not having anyone above him. It was self-contained; the flat below had their entrance at the opposite end of the building.

He nodded, signing on the pro-offered line, writing out a cheque for the first month's rent plus a deposit of the same amount there and then, shaking hands with Graham.

Graham promised to have the keys ready, with the details of the gas, water and electric companies for the following day. Indeed, he could bring the keys to Impervious if that suited Jason?

Jason nodded, beaming at him ecstatically, unable to believe his good fortune. Graham followed him out, locking the door securely behind him, offering him a lift to wherever he was going.

Jason realised that he was yet to answer Georgie's message, knowing she would be waiting for a reply. He thanked but declined Graham's offer, watching as he soon disappeared with the cheque securely in his pocket. Then he dialled Georgie's number, glad to find her quite calm, suggesting that they meet in this part of town, giving her the Tube station and promising to meet her in thirty minutes. He knew it would take twenty minutes' travelling from where she was, but he always allowed a little grace where public transport was concerned.

Georgie laughed to herself, rereading what she had written, marvelling at her own handiwork. She wouldn't dare show anyone the piece, but she could see how people became erotic authors and enjoyed it.

Looking up as the train stopped at the next station, she calculated how many stops remained: three. She reapplied her lip gloss, running her fingers through her already-smooth hair. Thoughts were running through her mind just like a train: her parents; her results; the girls; him; his new place and the search; their relationship; her questions over her career; but ultimately, the fact that she was in love with him. When her exams were over, she was free. She so desperately wanted this freedom.

The purpose of meeting him was to plan their relationship; to discover how he felt about her - and to find out if she was losing her heart for nothing. She swallowed hard. This was her friends' fault - they'd been egging her on for months; they had succeeded in moulding her into band material and under Jason's wing.

They'd coaxed and encouraged her, supplying her with a new wardrobe, improved confidence and tales of their own exploits, some of which sounded so whimsical it was all she could do but laugh. Georgie sighed.

The train slowed to Hammersmith station and the platform was already heaving with a mix of partygoers, tourists and workers. Georgie realised then that she'd expected a fairy tale - for the station to be empty and Jason to have roses in his arms and a grin on his face, waiting to throw his arms around her and whirl her around, as they did in the movies.

She sighed again, positively *crawling* along the carriage and then the platform, being swept along with the tide of people heading for the station exit. Unbuttoning her coat pocket, she took out her travel card, flashing it over the reader, allowing her out into the cool evening air, her gaze scanning for him.

Tall and short; fat and skinny; nice and dodgy-looking men: but no Jason. She side-stepped the crowd, slipping her phone from her pocket, checking the time and then checking she'd not missed any messages. She hadn't. It was 8.32 precisely, but he wasn't here.

Nervously she chewed her lip, gazing again at the time, unaware of the scruffy homeless man at her side until he was breathing in her ear. Georgie shuddered, the man's alcohol-infused breath hot on her cheek, barely hearing his plea for money. She shook her head and took a few steps away, cursing her luck. At that moment, her phone rang.

To her relief, Jason's number came up on the screen; pressing 'answer' and turning away from another crowd surging from the station, she was unable to see the homeless man engaging others.

"Hi, where are you? Is the train delayed?" Jason was scanning the steady stream of trains and travellers, unable to see her.

"I'm here, I'm outside! Where are *you*, more like?" She shuddered, huddling into her coat.

She could hear the confusion in his voice. "You're where?" Georgie rolled her eyes. As she was about to speak again, a sign caught her eye - she groaned. Turning, she saw the back of him across the road at another station entrance. She had to laugh at the irony of the situation; confusing Jason even more. "Stay where you are, I can see you, don't move."

She could hear the smile in his voice now. "How come you can see me, yet I can't see you?" She could see him turning, right and left, scrutinising the passengers as they filed past him.

"There's two bloody entrances!" Georgie laughed, despite her earlier annoyance. "You're at one and I'm at the other!"

Jason too laughed and Georgie shut off the connection, smiling to see him turn almost a full circle before he saw her and waved.

WHEN THE SAX MAN PLAYS PART 1 MAKING IT
Chapter 18

Jason brought his lunch with him the following day, skipping his usual treat of a home-cooked bar meal, hovering in Music Room 1 by the telephone, knowing any minute Graham would arrive and Reception would call for him to receive his visitor. They were very strict about visitors here: under no circumstances would Graham be allowed to enter the Music section, so Jason would have to make the journey to his guest.

After last night, he had another reason to smile. Their heart-to-heart had lasted three hours, and being the gentleman that he was, he had insisted on escorting Georgie home at that late hour, parting with longing looks as the Tube whisked him back to his single life. He smiled: not for much longer.

Their chosen bar was close by, and they had walked virtually past his new apartment on the way there. Informing her of his decision, he delighted in the way she skipped up the steps and leant against the glass, peering into the dark. He had laughed then and he laughed now.

He had been taken aback when she boldly revealed her feelings for him, wishing that he too was brave enough to declare his innermost emotions. This bright, fun, lovely young lady was putty in his hands *so easily*; he had done nothing, well virtually nothing to encourage her, and yet love had cast it's spell. He'd shaken his head, unable to believe his ears - yet so very thankful that this was not a dream.

He winced recalling how his side of the conversation had gone; containing none of her fluency, confidence or clarity. Her total honesty and belief in him rendered him speechless, and when he did find his tongue, he had stuttered and blushed. *Damn!*

Shrill ringing brought his attention back to the present: it was the phone call he had been waiting for. He left his untouched coffee steaming gently beside his half-eaten sandwich, bounding to his destination, a huge grin plastered across his face.

Graham shook his hand, enquiring after his health as was polite, handing over a folder and two keys with the rental agency's fob attached, before bidding him happiness, getting him to promise to call with any queries before hopping back down the steps and into his flashy sports car. Jason sighed jealousy watching him leave, but the emotion was soon lost to joy: the keys imprinting into his palm, such was the strength of his grip. The key to the continuing happiness of his own life!

"What timing you have." Christopher teased, wearily rubbing his eyes as he spoke.

"You sound tired, did you have hard day at the office?" Jason watched his brother's face change from a smile to a frown and back again as he laughed at the old joke they often shared.

"You could say that." Christopher took a deep breath. "I'm free tonight if you want to come round."

It wasn't a question, Jason realised, it was a statement. He smiled. "No, thanks, but I do have something to ask you." He noticed that Christopher suddenly sat up straighter. "Are you free for a midnight flit?"

Christopher groaned, but he was smiling. "You can't have a new pad already?"

Jason's beam was enough to convince him of the truth.

"Well I can hardly refuse, can I?" His eyes were twinkling now and Jason felt the relief wash over him, glad that his brother was back to his normal self. "I do instead on you wining and dining me first though."

"Oh." Jason's face fell.

"Are you skint from the deposit?" Christopher teased.

Jason laughed. "Not yet, no; I have two beans to rub together." He took a breath. "We have practice tonight, so can we make it nine thirty?"

Christopher swore. "You weren't kidding about the midnight part, were you?" He groaned, playfully hiding his head in his hands.

Over afternoon coffee, a brilliant idea struck Jason. He'd been reviewing his own music, feeling guilty that it had been weeks since his last performance at Fats. He missed it; he knew also his friends would want to hear how the bands were getting on, and he had their tickets in his desk drawer, as promised. The only problem was time - he had none!

Tonight he needed time with the bands; time with his brother; time to move and time to sleep. He also needed time away from another meeting with the blonde: that was the tricky part.

The idea came to him in a flash, as inspiration often does. He would go to Fats between finishing band practice and meeting Christopher, put to his proposal to Glenn that he and the groups take a set on Sunday night, and on his way out give him the envelope containing the tickets! Jason congratulated himself on such an efficient plan, brought back from his thoughts as the first of his last class of the day arrived noisily in the room.

Jason shut the door noisily behind him, knowing by now that this brought silence to the room - even with the bands. He had no desire to hear who the 'beautiful lay' Kipper was talking about was; his ears had failed to detect the quiet conversation going on between Vince, Michael and Georgie. His eyes sparkled when Georgie's gaze found his.

"Let's get on with it, shall we?" He looked around, ensuring he had their attention. "I'm in the midst of planning both groups a local gig, and I want to leave sharp to make the confirmations before I tell you all the how's and when's." He took in their collective looks of astonishment and awe - and Dave's fear. "It'll be great for your confidence." Dave tried to hide his laugh, but Jason ignored it. "Both groups are up to that standard, surprisingly fast." He made the admittance, sitting down in front of them. "The public appearance will boost morale in a way that I cannot." Again he paused. "I hope we're all up for it?" Everyone nodded, smiling; looking at each other in disbelief.

WHEN THE SAX MAN PLAYS PART 1 MAKING IT

"You really think we could hold a stage?" Dave's quavering voice rose above the self-congratulations.

"You already hold a stage - and nobody say the competition isn't real, of course it is. We all know that it's hotting up, and that's a sure sign we're in something serious, is it not?" Jason looked at Dave, who looked surprised, as if the thought had only just sunk in. He nodded, before Jason continued. "We have one, two, three," Jason counted the days on his fingers, "practices before the Quarterfinals. What do you want to work on?"

"I think we're fluent." Kipper said smugly, crossing his arms in front of his chest.

Jason fought to not roll his eyes. "Go on then." He smiled to himself, unusually giving in to Kipper.

"Go on then what?" Kipper frowned.

"Show us." Jason waved him towards a keyboard. "Play us through, then Michael can join you after the first chorus, then Dave, then Vince, then we'll play the final verse as a group."

"Why?" Kipper's eyes narrowed suspiciously.

"The best musicians can play their songs front to back, no backing support, no song sheet. Some practice blindfold."

"No way!" Michael laughed, taking in Jason's serious face.

Jason got to his feet. "If I can, then you can."

"You can play *blindfold*?" Vince gasped, stunned by the idea.

"You play with your eyes closed, it's the same thing." Jason replied.

Vince blushed as the room's attention focused on him.

WHEN THE SAX MAN PLAYS PART 1 MAKING IT

"You *what*?" Kipper spat.

"It blocks out all the distractions so I can concentrate better." Vince shrugged almost apologetically, unable to explain further. It was a new feeling for him, seeing respect slipping into their expressions as his band mates looked at him in awe. He consigned the moment to memory, sure that it wouldn't happen often!

"Who wants to tie the blindfold?" As if by magic, Jason had a silk handkerchief in his hands.

Kipper beat everyone else to it, bounding over to him and securing the knot tightly in no time.

"Don't cut off my circulation!" Jason joked, glad when the room laughed. He groped beside him for his saxophone, deciding to play the tune to "Say What You Want"; the very song that he said the saxophone piece would be difficult to play.

It soon became obvious that Jason had been practising. He wished he could see Georgie's face, knowing she would be completely lost in the music. It was an interesting trait most of his students displayed, and it gave him great joy to watch their expressions as they were entranced by their favourite piece.

"Play another!" Michael demanded. "Play mine!"

Jason nodded, taking a deep breath before commencing. He mocked bowed three minutes later after an equally perfect second performance. "Now, can someone please untie me?" He laughed, not wanting to risk putting down the saxophone without looking.

Georgie reached him first, putting one hand around his on the saxophone, guiding it to rest safely on the stand before untying Kipper's knot. She joked about the tightness of the knot, glad that she had nails to use!

Jason too laughed, but was suddenly aware that the room's attention was on the pair. As the atmosphere clouded, he could almost hear their brains whirring. "Thank you Georgie. Now c'mon Kipper, show us what you've got, we know you're good but how perfect are you?" He sat down, virtually able to see the steam pouring from Kipper's ears. He laughed to himself, unable to see behind him that Vince and Michael too were sharing a grin, hearing someone whisper that it served him right, but not able to put a name to the voice.

Jason found himself in the Union Bar waiting for Dave for their usual impromptu Monday morning meeting. A smile settled on his face.

The weekend had flown by, but had been full of surprises and joys. Their late dinner at Christopher's choice of restaurant had been exceptional; Jason had kept the wine bottle hovering by his brother's side, sensing that he needed the release. Christopher's shoulders slumped from the weight of the world resting there; an hour later, Jason had restored him to his usual jolly self. They had roared with laughter more than once at Jason's meeting with Georgie at Hammersmith station.

Jason looked back, glad that he could laugh now. The ensuing conversation had given him more than a few pointers. He had paid the taxi fare to his flat, dragging a jokingly reluctant Christopher up the steps, pleased to see the blonde was absent.

An hour later, they realised there necessitated another taxi to Hammersmith. Jason had a suitcase and his saxophone; with Christopher carrying another case and a large box, which he couldn't see either over or round, which made negotiating the steps dangerous. They'd both laughed as he'd staggered and sworn, both feeling more cheery than usual thanks to the restaurant's excellent Rioja.

"What's happening with this second song then?" Dave's voice cut through Jason's reminiscing. His worried expression reached Jason long before he took his seat.

"I told you, let's get through the Quarterfinals first." Jason said, putting his reassurance mode on overdrive. He *had* hoped that Dave's confidence would grow as the band progressed, wondering what was in his background that afforded him no self-belief. "Now, c'mon, what's on your mind?"

"Nothing." Dave spoke rather quickly.

"There must be something. You're an accomplished guitarist now, you have many successful auditions behind you. Remember that buzz we feel when we're on stage?" Jason paused, waiting while he nodded. "Maybe it'll help to recall those memories, those magical feelings, at the times you feel it's all too much." Dave smiled, but it was an ironic smile. "Every waking hour?" Jason's relaxed expression sobered in an instant. The counselling part of his training flashed through his mind. "What makes you say that? What's going on at home?"

Dave shook his head slowly. "You wouldn't understand." His voice fell.

"Try me." Jason softened his voice equally.

Dave shook his head again, and to Jason's horror he saw him blink tears away. Dave fought against his immediate reaction to flee, wondering if he could summon some courage to let out those painful, jumbled feelings.

After a few minutes, he tried his voice. "I know I should feel good, I should feel confident." His fists clenched tightly on the table and his eyes were squeezed closed as he spoke. "I can't." He shook his head sorrowfully, causing the tears to leak past his eyelashes. "I'm a failure. I always have been, and I always will be."

"What?" Jason gasped. "No Dave, you're not a failure!" Forgetting where they were for a moment, he squeezed Dave's hands, not caring who saw them and potentially got the wrong idea. "Listen to me." He gripped Dave's hands tightly. "I don't know who's put that idea in your head, but it's lies. Horrible lies." He repeated. "It'll only become true if you let it Dave, and I know you won't let that happen." He squeezed again before taking his hands back, glad that his reaction had been well received; glad also that his touch had the desired effect on Dave's shaken demeanour.

"My family have no faith in me." Dave struggled to control his wavering voice. "They constantly tell me I'm not good enough; and that I'll never get a decent job, or a decent grade. They think I'm wasting my time here. They were surprised when I was accepted, and they're surprised I haven't been kicked off the course yet." He snorted. "They don't know about the band."

"What?" Jason gasped, aware that he was starting to sound like a broken record.

Dave was still shaking his head. "I can't tell them, they'll laugh, and..." he took a deep breath, "...they'll try'n stop me."

"You're a grown man Dave, they can't stop you from doing anything." Jason reasoned. In that second, he saw himself in Dave, all the more empowered by his own success. "All it takes is a little confidence. You need to have faith in yourself."

Dave again laughed that ironic laugh.

Jason leant across the table, catching his eye. "I'm going to tell you something about me; something I don't want you to tell anyone else." When Dave locked eyes with him, Jason knew that he was safe to tell him of his upbringing; of his parents' harsh attitude; of how he was still alienated, save from Christopher.

The only difference between the two situations was that Dave was an only child, but Jason pointed out that it wasn't a hurdle, not if he used it to his own advantage; pointing out that sooner or later his family would realise that he was all they had and then, they would make amends. Alas, his story did not have the same forecasted happy ending.

Chapter 19

Jason stretched, echoes of the alarm still ringing in his ears. He couldn't believe it was morning already; worse still, he had to get up earlier thanks to a longer commute to Impervious. He sighed.

But it was worth it, he reminded himself as he got up: it was worth a three hour commute, he smiled wryly, glad that in forty minutes he'd be walking into Impervious from the nearest Underground station.

He studied his reflection in the mirror. Christopher, albeit slightly the worse for wear after that three-quarter bottle's worth of Rioja, had commented on his brother's sallow complexion, telling him that he needed a woman, momentarily forgetting. Jason had paused and Christopher latched onto the meaning of the silence.

"Well!" He slapped Jason's back. "Why aren't you happy?"
Jason had laughed, he remembered. "I am happy, it's just that we can't officially see each other for a few weeks."
Christopher had groaned. "It's typical of you to fall for a bloody student!"

"Georgie is not a 'bloody student' - she'll qualify in six weeks."
Christopher had snorted then. "I suppose she's a bloody massage beauty therapist?"
Jason shook his head. "She's a trainee lawyer, she's got a position lined up at MacMillan's."
Christopher's eyes had opened wide; he began then to dig for

more information but Jason was like a closed book. He apologised, fixing something to sober himself up with before quizzing Jason again.

A further hour later, Jason encouraged Christopher to take the spare room, before he remembered there was no bed. He was amused to see Christopher lying on the floor, one blanket over him, one underneath him not five minutes later, already snoring.

Red wine had that effect on him... Jason smiled to himself, closing over the door again. He'd managed to only impart the basics about Georgie, but he knew Christopher wouldn't settle for less than everything he knew, and felt, once he was sober!

Friday nights' memories were still crystal clear in his mind, Jason found himself replaying their conversation as he washed and dressed. He then attempted to make a cup of tea, before he remembered that he hadn't got a kettle, never mind tea bags or milk.

Settling on toast to sustain him until his arrival at Impervious, he opened the cupboard, hooking out the loaf, only to discover it was mouldy. He touched the shelf, finding it damp. He groaned, his eye tracing the line of cupboard shelves, the telltale damp spot spreading across the ceiling tiles. He swore then, picking up his jacket and saxophone, grabbing his bag en-route, ensuring the door firmly locked behind him, trying to ignore his growling stomach.

An attractive young lady boarded the train at the next stop, cradling a takeaway cup of coffee and a warm pastry. Jason blushed as a particularly loud growl rose from his complaining stomach upon being presented with the delectable smells, but thankfully nobody seemed to notice.

She smiled at him and Jason smiled back. He wished he had something to read to pass the journey, left with nothing to do except stare into space, watching his fellow travellers and wondering about their lives.

Some people were quite easy to read: the tourists with their guidebooks talking in their excitable chatter; the students with their bulging book bags, constantly ringing mobile phones and the smell of their takeaway breakfasts wafting through the carriages; the businessmen in their sombre suits, orderly briefcases by their side; the mums out to shop and take the kids to school were the stressed ones, constantly telling off the young kids around them, checking their watches, wondering if their schedule was going to work today?

Jason realised he was none of these stereotypes. He looked at himself: smart-casual dark trousers, navy jumper with a pale blue shirt beneath it, boring black slip-on shoes and corresponding rain jacket; over-shoulder bag and bulging saxophone case. His short flame-red hair was immaculate, a regular four-week trim ensured it was kept under control. His hands were soft but supple, his nails trimmed short, his classic gentleman's watch peering out from his left sleeve.

But what about his face? Christopher thought he looked pale, ill almost, what word had he used: sallow? That wasn't good. He caught his reflection in the Underground's darkened windows, looking past the attractive brunette with the now half-eaten pastry and empty coffee cup. He did look pale; he was astonished to see ghostly purple circles under his eyes. The eyes themselves were bright with anticipation for what the day would bring.

He had been blessed with a normal face, with a smattering of freckles as bemoaned people with his colouring; eyebrows that weren't too unruly and teeth that were naturally white. He was slender build, but of an average height.

The brunette laughed loudly, bringing Jason's attention to her, expecting her to be talking on her mobile. He was surprised to find that she was looking directly at him. The blush started without warning, creeping its inevitable way up neck to his face.

"Do you often stare at strangers?" She joked.

"Sorry," Jason's blush deepened, "it's not personal." He looked around them, seeing the carriage was half empty, everyone else either engrossed in their paper or listening to music, lost in their own private world. He wondered whether to say something else, and he knew she was still looking at him: when his gaze returned, she locked eyes with him.

"I haven't seen you here before." She teased, smiling at him.

"Do you come here often?" Jason laughed when she did.

"It's a boring daily commute." She confided in him, having regarded him in quiet contemplation for a moment or two. "Will you be making it regularly?"

"I will." Jason nodded. "Weekdays, heading to work."

"In the City, or just passing through?"

Jason nodded. "Inner City. How about you?"

"Same." Her eyes twinkled; her gaze ran over his saxophone case. "Are you a musician?"

Jason laughed. "Close enough, I'm a Music tutor. I'd love to be a professional." He sighed wistfully.

"Tutor or musician?" She joked.

"Both!" Jason laughed, glad when she too laughed. He saw her gaze then sweep over his hands, hovering over his left hand. Her smile was triumphant, he was sure.

"I'm Sabrina."

"I'm Jason." He smiled back at her, wondering if this was how his daily commute was going to play out. A thought struck him: would such behaviour constitute flirting? If so, shouldn't he avoid this, as he was spoken for?

"Well, it's been lovely meeting you Jason, but I must alight." She gave a little giggle. "We'll go further tomorrow. I have an early appointment before work. Same time, same place?"

Jason nodded. "Sure. Have a nice day, Sabrina."

"And you, Jason - go and make beautiful music." With that, the train juddered to a halt and Sabrina disappeared into the crowd.

Kipper moaned. "Maya is *killing* me over Ericka!"

Dave frowned, confused, sure that it was too early to be dealing with Kipper's mind-games. He stirred his coffee. "Who's

Ericka?"

"Ericka is the hottest babe you've ever seen."

Dave nodded. "I can see Maya's point, knowing your track record!"

Kipper shrugged. "She's playing the leading lady, I have to get closer to her for the good of the performance."

"The same sleazy way you are around Georgie?" Dave observed, taking a sip of his coffee and burning his tongue.

"I don't sleaze over anyone." Kipper frowned at him.

"You hardly leave her alone, I'm surprised you remember about Jason and I at all."

"You're just jealous!" Kipper shouted, getting to his feet. "Geez Dave! Ask her out, don't take your frustrations out on me!" He hurried off, leaving Dave alone, shaking his head in disbelief.

Silently he pitied Maya, Kipper's girlfriend, knowing they had only been together a short time and already Kipper's attention had wandered. It didn't say much for the state of their so-called relationship, did it? Dave knew his friend was obsessed with what Kipper called 'totty' - the very word made Dave wince. He foresaw his friend going through every gorgeous girl in London and still not finding someone special, not that he was trying or looking, it was just how he functioned.

Suddenly Dave was thankful that he was normal. He smiled thinking back to his conversation with Jason, knowing deep down that he was right. Somewhere, there was a light at the end of the tunnel, he just had to find it...

Perhaps Kipper was right though; he did like Georgie. He didn't want to ruin anything between them, so perhaps after the competition was over and while emotions were running high, perhaps then he could pluck up the courage to ask her to dinner? He downed the rest of his now-cold coffee, making his way to his first class of the day.

Jason unlocked the doors: Music Room 1 first, then Room 2, then the smaller storage room. He set out the text books by each desk, flicking on the power switch at the wall, casting his eye over the room and everything therein. It always gave him a little inward thrill, knowing that all he surveyed was his own.

This was worth the hard work; the hours of concentration and practice; the sneaking out to explore the world of music around him that had previously been out of his reach. *This* was worth enduring his family criticisms.

He was looking forward to breaking the good news to both bands tonight - their gig at Fats Jazz Club was arranged for the following Sunday evening.

Kipper's soft knock on the door met no reply, so he knocked louder and Jason looked up.

"I won't make practice tonight."

Jason spun round in his chair to face Kipper, who was leaning against the door, looking stressed and exhausted. "You'd better have a good reason. It's not too late to kick you out."

WHEN THE SAX MAN PLAYS PART 1 MAKING IT

"You wouldn't."

"Do you want to try me?" Jason's solemn expression set and he held Kipper's gaze. "Sit down and tell me what's happening." Kipper hesitated, then he realised that it was an order. He slunk into the room, sinking into the chair opposite Jason, feeling his gaze burning into him. "I have to be with Maya."

"Maya," Jason repeated, slowly, thinking...

"My girlfriend." Kipper paused. "Ex-girlfriend."

"Ex-girlfriend?" Jason repeated again, leaning back in his chair. "You need to start at the beginning, I don't follow." He steepled his fingers in front of his face, his elbows resting on the arms of the chair, allowing silence to fall between them. "It'll have to be quick, I have a class in ten minutes."

Kipper nodded. He met Jason's gaze, allowing his eyes to drop to the floor once more. Whatever it was, Jason recognised it was hard for him to say.

"She's pregnant." Kipper's voice, usually so bold, came out a whisper.

"Ah." The word hung between them. Hundreds of questions buzzed around Jason's head, but he kept quiet.

"I'm going with her, to the doctors, for the confirmation." He swallowed hard, finally lifting his gaze from the floor but still unable to look Jason in the eye.

"That's admirable of you." Jason spoke carefully, keeping his tone neutral.

Kipper's angry gaze shot to his face. "What the fuck does that mean?"

"You don't believe her, so you want to go along and make sure it's the truth?" Jason tried to keep the disgust out of his voice.

Kipper's voice changed from angry to forlorn. "What can I do?"

"How about believe her, and support her." Jason rolled his eyes. "There comes a time when you can no longer live a selfish, carefree life. Sometimes it's earlier in life than you anticipated, but everything happens for a reason. You should do the decent thing and stand by this poor girl."

"It takes two to tango." Kipper began, as if to shift some of the blame to Maya.

"Exactly!" Jason crossed his arms over his chest.

Another silence fell between them.

"I'll come back after the appointment, but it might be a bit late."

"Better late than never." Jason's parting words remained with Kipper for the rest of the afternoon.

Georgie crept quietly into the room, tiptoeing behind Jason, putting her hands over his eyes and giggling. She apologised when he jumped, smiling when he swung round in the chair, grabbing hold of her as she squealed.

This close, she could smell the faint trace of his aftershave, mingling with her freshly applied Gucci. She stroked his face tenderly as they kissed, holding his kiss before pulling away.

"When am I getting to see your new place, properly?" She teased, sitting down in the nearest chair.

Jason was lost in the smell of her, desperate for a second to have her alone, and in private. He suppressed the urge, but it was getting harder to quash.

"I don't know if it's yet up to your high standard." He teased.

"Knowing you, it's perfect already." Georgie purred, leaning in towards him.

Jason made the man's fatal mistake of taking his eyes from her face, his attention drawn to the way that her blouse was coming undone...

"You said you didn't want 'us' to officially begin until you'd graduated." He managed to choke the words out, sweat beading his upper lip.

"Only for your sake." Georgie licked her lips, teasing him. "But we can still have fun as friends, can't we?"

Jason shook his head. "I don't think friends have naughty thoughts about each other, do they?" He spoke softly, licking his own lips and wanting to kiss her, watching her face soften as she laughed.

He knew the other band members would be arriving any second now, half wanting someone to appear now, but half not wanting to be interrupted.

"What about Sunday?" Georgie offered.

Jason shook his head. "Saturday is free, are you free?" She nodded, her smile encouraging him. "A candlelit dinner for two, at my place, how does that sound?"

"Do friends have candlelit dinners?" Georgie teased, pleased when he laughed. She got up, crossing the room to his saxophone, which sat proud as ever on it's stand in the corner. Jason watched the way she caressed it's neck, feeling jealous of the instrument.

"What are you doing to that saxophone?" Vince teased her, the second he arrived.

"It's a beautiful instrument." Georgie murmured.

"Do you regularly stroke instruments?" He continued to tease, sharing a joking look with Jason.

"Not as often as I'd like to." Georgie admitted.

Jason closed his eyes, revelling in that thought for a moment.

"Okay, this is getting too involved for me now!" Vince laughed.

"What's happening?" Michael arrived at that moment, sitting in his usual place opposite Jason, smiling at him.

The crisp sheets were the opposite of the peachy-softness of her skin, but the carefully thought out details were lost on him as he pushed her onto the bed, groping and kissing her, unable to get enough of her. Their breathing becoming more and more laboured as the intensity grew. Butterfly kisses drew her down his perfectly toned body to his proud manhood, fully erect for her inspection. She cupped his bulge, kissing his firm shaft.

Suddenly she switched the movements, her hand gripping the base of his shaft, rubbing up and down, up and down, making him harder still; making him sweat and moan. She gasped as his fingers found the inside of her, thrusting deeply, almost painfully, rhythmically, bringing her to the edge of orgasm, stopping just as she was about to be engulfed by the waves of pleasure.

Frustrated, she abandoned her own plan of action, straddling his firm body and sliding down onto him, fully engulfing him. With every hip thrust, her breasts danced; his hands guiding them, bringing her nipples to his mouth, to suck and tease them, biting them as she climaxed, caught in simultaneous orgasm as they achieved the sweet release together.

Georgie was amazed how the piece had flowed through her fingers to the keyboard, as if writing itself. She hoped sex with Jason would be equally as hot; she rather fancied slow, sensual lovemaking but she didn't really know what to expect.

She hoped he was a passionate lover, selfless and willing to try anything. One day she might even fulfil her wildest sexual fantasy with him... She gave a shudder of anticipation with the thought.

Chapter 20

Jason smiled as Sabrina sat opposite him as she had done the previous day, returning his smile and saying 'good morning'. The look in her eye was mischievous: Jason wondered what it meant.

"Surely if you're a tutor you don't need to carry your instrument in every day?" She said, over a slurp of coffee.

Jason noticed a few eyebrows were raising in the adjacent seats. He laughed. "That's true, but I'm not comfortable without it."

Sabrina raised an eyebrow, inquisitively. "Why? Don't your doors have locks?"

Jason sighed. "Unfortunately that isn't enough."

Her eyes widened. "You've already had a break-in?"

Jason nodded. "I guess I have enemies."

Sabrina laughed. "How on Earth can *you* make enemies? It's the impolite, bad-mannered people who have that blessing."

Jason shrugged, blushing with the compliment. "I must be special." He added as an afterthought, trying to joke, though the whole recent situation still stung.

Sabrina jumped straight on it. "I'll say you are." She regarded him carefully. "You don't seem like a pigheaded, self-centred man either." She added, batting her eyelashes at him.

Jason wondered if this was his cue to tell her that he was already spoken for, when she jumped in before him.

"Unlike my boyfriend." She sighed.

"Your boyfriend?" Jason repeated.

"I'm attractive enough to have a boyfriend, aren't I?" She treated him to a full-on beam to show that she wasn't offended.

"Of course! Everyone deserves happiness." He paused. "Does he make you happy?"

She shrugged, taking another slurp of her coffee.

"I'm sorry, I shouldn't have asked." Jason held his hands up in apology. "Change the subject. Whereabouts do you work?"

"Victoria, in the shopping arcade by the coach station. I own the lingerie boutique." There was a pause as she finished her coffee. "I design them myself."

"Wow." Jason couldn't think of a suitable reply, having never known anyone in the fashion industry, never mind in lingerie... He hoped his one word would suffice, relieved when it did.

Sabrina laughed. "At least if I get someone nasty I eject them from the premises, what do you do with unruly students?"

Jason smiled. "We do the same. There's nothing worse than a student who doesn't want to be in a class." He shook his head. "Eight weeks in, we eject them!" He smiled at her. "From then on, it's plain sailing."

Sabrina pulled a face. "You mean it's boring?"

"Oh no, not at all." Jason grinned thinking about the battle of bands, and his few truly gifted students who would go on to greater things. "I like a challenge as much as the next man."

"Is that so?" Sabrina smiled at him. "Tell me about your latest challenge."

So the journey was filled with talk of the Annual Talent Contest,

and how the other tutors had blackmailed the Music students.
How she gasped! He went on to talk about Miracle - cool name
she interrupted - and how Georgie's Guys had formed as a
breakaway group. He told her about the Quarterfinals, in two
days time!, and was surprised when she asked if there were still
tickets available...?

"We are booked for our first gig on Sunday evening, as you
know." Jason paused. "I wondered how we all felt about that,"
he paused again, scanning their faces, taking in their nods, "and
about starting on our second song?"
He expected Dave to look horrified, but not the rest of them.
Kipper shrugged, no doubt still under a cloud regarding what
had gone on previously in the doctor's office. Jason didn't want
to interfere, nor bring attention to this fact in front of the group,
as Kipper had sworn him to secrecy; knowing also that Kipper
would come to him if he wanted to continue the conversation. It
was amazing that his loose schedule which he had cursed when
he had begun, had worked out so well for those in need of him.
Jason smiled to himself.
"Guys, the enthusiasm is killing you all!" He sat down in front of
them. "Let's give it a try." He took a deep breath. "We need to
have it off pat by three weeks' time either way."
Dave groaned, burying his head in his hands.
But Vince was nodding. "I'm ready for the challenge." He gave
Jason a wide beam, which confused the rest of the band.

WHEN THE SAX MAN PLAYS PART 1 MAKING IT

Nobody else knew of the plan that the pair had hatched the previous day in one phone call. Vince had offered his services to Jason when he'd heard about the second song - he'd surrendered his lunch hours to take to the drums to learn Jason's part in Georgie's Guys, admitting that it was quite easy to switch from one tune to another. He'd agreed to take over the drumming for the second song for Georgie's Guys, as Jason's plan included a solo spell on the saxophone. The grateful glint in Jason's eyes was worth the sacrifice, in Vince's opinion.

"Count us in." Georgie said, nodding with Michael, both of them grinning at Jason.

"I need all the practice I can get." Dave admitted, foreseeing practice sessions every night, with or without the band.

Jason's gaze landed on Kipper, who sighed. "I'll take that as a yes?" He tried. "Good of the group and all that?" Still Kipper didn't move or agree. "Or I can just cut you out - your choice." Kipper got to his feet, albeit reluctantly.

Dave swallowed hard. "How do you know that I won't start playing the other song tomorrow night?" He looked around them - they were in their usual seat in the Union Bar later that evening, just the two of them. Aware they were performing again the next night, Dave wondered if the time was going a little too quickly...

"Dave, don't worry, please. You know you'll be fine." Jason shook his head, along with Dave. "You *will* be fine. Look at it this way: when Miracle are on, you play the right song, and when you play with Georgie's Guys, you play the other song. You'll automatically play the right song." He saw the pleading look haunting Dave's pale face. "I wish I could convince you." Jason spoke honestly, looking into his eyes. "One day, you too will find your own way in life. As you gain experience, you will gain confidence and faith in yourself. You need to take whatever opportunity comes your way, though." He paused, reading the young man's expression as he sat puzzled but interested in front of him. "Like College. Your tutors all say how polite and conscientious you are; how you are a hardworking, dedicated academic who they foresee faring well in the final examinations." Dave's mouth hung open. "You... you spoke to them?"

Jason nodded. It was technically a white lie... Hamish had said so himself, and nobody knew the tutors' thoughts better than the Principal. "Don't let it make you bigheaded!" He joked, glad when Dave laughed with him. "Also, your commitment to the band is immense. We would be lost without you. None of us are perfect Dave, and we all need to work together. I know I can trust you to give your best performance; to rehearse properly; to give your input whenever it is called upon." Jason smiled at him. "Look at Kipper - how much trouble he causes me!" They both laughed again. "And Vince - remember the sessions he missed when he went AWOL with his new girlfriend? I just don't have these problems with you - I know I can trust you. I'm so glad there's one stable influence amongst us."

Dave frowned, trying to memorise Jason's compliments. "What

about Michael? He's reliable."

"Ah," Jason paused and his silence spoke volumes. "Reliable yet unpredictable. As a band member I have no issues with him."

"There's just something you can't put your finger on?" Dave offered.

Jason smiled wryly. "Something like that, yes."

Sabrina's beaming smile was the first thing he was aware of that morning on the journey to Impervious.

"Nervous?" She chuckled, seeing Jason's paler than usual face.

Jason smiled and then sighed. "I don't know why! I perform solo regularly and I don't feel this amount of butterflies *ever*."

"You're nervous for everyone else." Sabrina suggested, shrugging her shoulders, but he was shaking his head.

"They're nervous enough without me!" He laughed again.

"I believe that." She paused, regarding him carefully. "What will you do if only one of them gets a place in the Semis?"

The question disarmed him a little, he had to admit, and he pondered it through the morning; pondering also the answer that he had given to a carriage of open ears.

Chapter 21

He laughed at himself, realising that he was behaving like a cat on a hot tin roof. He paced the room; working his students harder and demanding more from them. Unusually, he didn't see any of either band's members at lunch, not even in passing. Only a nod from Michael in the afternoon made him smile for the last few *torturous* hours of the day's classes.

He had a good group of students, some of which he could see winning competitions just like the Impervious Annual. It was a complete waste that they weren't entered. But still, he smiled to himself again, the challenge had brought together the two bands he now managed. The thought struck him that it would soon be over... and what would he do then?

He pondered this thought over his coffee, half an eye on the clock. Hamish had called him for a meeting at five, an hour before the Quarterfinals began. A ripple of immediate suspicion flooded his mind, but it could be completely innocent. Hamish knew that Jason would be there, so it made sense... He shook his head with his thoughts, knowing the events were connected.

He began the long walk to Hamish's office at 4.50 pm, feeling like he was going to meet his maker. He shook himself, laughing at his own silliness. He was taken aback to see Hamish standing in the doorway of his office, waiting for him. The Principal didn't greet him normally - gone was the warm handshake and a huge, genuine smile - instead ushering him inside and closing the door furtively. Jason could feel the shake beginning in his legs, a sure sign that all was not well.

Numbly Jason sat down amongst the bands, squeezed into their usual booth in the Union Bar, thirty minutes after his short meeting with Hamish.

"Jason? What's wrong?" Georgie's voice startled him back to the present.

He looked around seeing everyone's attention was glued to him. Still speechless, he shook his head. They knew where he had been, and had been waiting for him, too nervous to concentrate on anything but tonight's competition; even Georgie, who was usually unshakeable.

"Get him a drink." Dave nudged Kipper, who was nearest the bar. "Something strong, he needs it."

Kipper nodded, and set off with purpose.

Jason closed his eyes, his head spinning, the same thought on auto-play through his mind. How could he tell them? But then, how could he not tell them?

"Hard liquor." Kipper banged down the glass on the table, causing the dark liquid to swish violently round the glass. "Get that down you and tell us what the hell's going on!" He pushed the glass into Jason's hand, sitting opposite him.

Slowly a smile crept over Jason's lips. Who would've thought that he *could* rely on Kipper to keep him steady?

"Drink." Kipper encouraged, pushing the glass further into his grip, seeing him remain still.

They all exchanged looks around the table.

 "They're not sacking you?" Michael spoke into the silence. Five pairs of eyes swivelled to his face. "It's not so dumb, he's been in with the Principal and now he's so shocked he can't speak." His theory met with a few nods.

Jason shook his head. "No." His voice cracked. Against his best intentions, he lifted the glass to his lips tentatively, and at the last second, took a mouthful. His eyes smarted as his throat caught fire: he choked and coughed.

Vince, who was sitting next to him, banged him on the back. "What're you trying to do - kill him?" He glared at Kipper, having an idea what the dark liquid had been - Smithy's lethal concoction from a bottle kept under the bar and only brought out in cases of extremity.

Still Jason coughed, trying to catch his breath. But it had worked - he was out of his fog now, despite the fact he couldn't think through the alcohol steaming through his veins!

Smithy himself appeared with a pint glass of water, also glaring at Kipper. "You should have warned him to sip!" He slapped Jason on the back a few times, forcing his hand around the water glass, gesturing for him to swallow the whole glass.

Never one to disobey an order, Jason did as he was told.

 "What time did you say you were on?" Smithy continued, looking around the table.

 "Six-thirty." Michael answered, smiling at him, his expression relieved as Jason stopped gasping.

"And eight forty." Georgie added.

"Shouldn't you be going? It's quarter to six now." Smithy laughed as the six got to their feet and left as one.

"Good evening ladies and gentlemen - and students." Hamish's opening speech began, making the room erupt into laughter. Everyone settled down. "We are here to see the Quarterfinalists of this year's Impervious Annual Talent Competition. This is the seventh consecutive year of our competition. As most of you who have witnessed these events before know, we often have an eventful Final." Hamish paused for effect. "However, this year proceedings will be different. I'm pleased to announce there will be a coveted prize."

Jason closed his eyes, knowing what was coming next.

"Are you alright?" Georgie whispered to him, giving his arm a squeeze.

He nodded, not trusting his voice, keeping his eyes closed.

"It is my pleasure to announce that this year's winner will land a professional recording contract." Hamish beamed, amongst the gasps and squeals of disbelief from the assembled crowd. He indicated the two cameras set up at the back of the auditorium. "Every stage of the competition has been recorded and will be broadcast on prime-time TV." Hamish's speech continued, wrapping up the audience in his words.

"Jason?" Vince gave him a nudge. "Are you okay?" He looked

past Jason, at Georgie, who was sitting on his opposite side. She shook her head. "C'mon, let's get some fresh air." He stood up, grabbing Jason's arm, glad when Georgie took his other arm. Michael and Dave began to protest, but Vince took charge, instructing them to come outside just before Miracle were called. Kipper nodded.

"We'll sit here, we're not far away." Vince sat on the low wall, still able to hear the noise in the auditorium. "A moment's peace." He looked meaningfully at Georgie over Jason's shoulder.

"Yes, that's a good idea." She smiled at him, noticing that he had his arm around Jason's shoulders, which meant there was no excuse for her not to show the same concern, wrapping her arm around his waist, giving him a little squeeze as she did so.

"Thanks guys," Jason put his hands over his eyes.

"It's okay, it's the shock, we all feel the same." Vince smiled at Georgie again.

"We're just glad you're not going to pass out on us." Georgie teased, glad when he laughed.

Jason swallowed. "No, no chance of that." He looked at both of them. "That was one lethal drink!"

They both laughed.

"Maybe you shouldn't take a drink from Kipper again." Vince said, testing Jason's reaction, smiling when he laughed.

"You knew, didn't you?" Georgie accused him. "About the contract."

Jason nodded. "I didn't know how to tell you all..." He took a deep breath, still able to feel where the pure alcohol had burned down his throat and through his chest.

"And we thought there was something wrong!" Vince laughed.

"There is." Jason turned to look at him. "Life will never be the same again for the winners."

"Why not?" Vince's frown was mirrored on Georgie's face.

"You'd be followed everywhere by fans. You'd be recognised everywhere you went, and you'd never get a moment's peace. You wouldn't have a normal life." He shook his head.

"All this from a recording contract?" Vince's eyes widened.

Jason nodded solemnly.

A serious, silent air hung between them.

"Who wants a normal life anyway?!" Vince laughed, glad when Jason and Georgie too laughed. "I'm here to bloody win this competition, I'm sure the rest of the band feel the same."

Jason took another deep breath. "But only one group will win."

"No kidding, Sherlock." Vince grinned. "How long did it take you to form that blinder?"

Georgie rolled her eyes. "What he means is," she paused, looking at Jason, "he doesn't know who is going to win, it might not be one of us, but it might be one of us - one over the other. How bloody awkward would that be?"

At that moment, Michael ran towards them. "We've been put back, we're on at seven."

Vince and Georgie both nodded, consulting their watches.

"The Principal wants you." Michael looked at Jason, taking in the fact that he wasn't about to keel over. "You're to make a speech."

"What?!" Jason exclaimed.

"You've got three minutes." Michael tugged at his arm, trying to get him to his feet.

Jason groaned, rubbing his head. "What am I going to say?"

"He's got it ready on the auto cue." Michael explained, glad when the three got to their feet and began to walk with him.

"Thank God for that." Jason sighed.

It seemed like seconds later, his name was announced and Hamish was beckoning him onstage. The crowd cheered and clapped; the noise almost drowned out by the sound of blood pounding in his ears. For the first time ever, Jason was aware how hot it was on stage.

Reaching the lectern, he took the microphone from Hamish, his eyes desperately searching for the auto cue monitor. He caught sight of his friends from Fats, which made him smile; spying also Christopher four rows in, who gave him a mock salute, and then just three rows along sat Sabrina, beaming widely at him. Several flashes went off from all over the auditorium. That was the last thing he remembered.

Someone was saying his name, over and over. Groggily, Jason was aware of other voices around him, dimly recalling where he was. Quick as a flash the memory hit him: he'd collapsed onstage at Hamish's opening ceremony. He groaned. Worse still; it was all on camera, and it would be broadcast to the nation. He groaned again.

"Steady." Christopher's serious voice warned him, his hand lightly on Jason's chest.

Jason moaned. "Please tell me I didn't do that."

Christopher looked up at Georgie, and the rest of the band. "He's fine." He chuckled, relieved.

"Don't worry, everyone's quite sympathetic." Georgie touched his nearest shoulder, smiling when Jason opened his eyes to look at her. "That was the best get-out clause I've seen in a long time." She joked. "Are you ready to sit up?"

Jason nodded, letting Christopher help him, moaning as his head spun. Georgie knelt behind him, getting him to lean back against her.

Christopher frowned. "I've never known him to pass out."

"I haven't." Jason took a shaky breath, feeling the room dim.

"This is not the time to start, y'know." Kipper joked, crouching down with them. He looked at Christopher. "This isn't my fault, is it?" The thought struck him like a blow. "It's not," he stopped.

"It's not what?" Christopher kept his voice level.

"Alcohol poisoning - doesn't that make you sick?" Kipper looked fearfully at Christopher, and around at the others. "I mean, he didn't have much, but what he had was strong."

Christopher's eyes narrowed. "How strong?" From the second he'd met the young man in front of him, he was struck with the notion that he exaggerated everything, but he *could* be serious if the occasion called for it.

Kipper shrugged. "Practically illegal, I reckon."

Christopher shook his head. A small voice in the back of his mind reminded him of the cases of students brought in with dangerously high levels of alcohol in their bloodstream.

"I'm fine." Jason squeezed his eyes shut, aware he was the centre of attention; aware that here his two worlds were merging. Here was his big brother looking after him, being protective of him as always. Jason was glad *someone* in the family cared about him, glad that he could count on Christopher - not that there had ever been any doubt about that in his mind. It seemed too that here his fellow band mates also cared about him. He knew Georgie did, but he had been taken aback by Vince's earlier compassion.

"You don't look fine." Georgie said, gently beginning to rub his back. "There's no way you can play like this."

"The show must go on." He spoke through gritted teeth.

The saying kicked up some nervous laughter in the room.

"You are *kidding*?" Dave touched his nearest shoulder. "Jason, there's no way..."

"I'll be fine as long as I'm concentrating on something." He took a deep breath. "It's probably just a virus." He waved his hand dissuasively, secretly fearing the idea that Kipper had planted in their heads. Hamish's news had come as a complete shock; his shock deepening as he was tipped to win; deepening further still

when Hamish told him to never look a gift horse in the mouth...
After that, he'd tuned out, unable to take in any more. Very
dimly in the background he was aware of the constantly changing
music. He shook his head. "How long have we got?"

"Ten minutes." Vince answered, consulting his watch. He turned
to the rest of the group, organising them as he'd seen Jason do
many times. "You can sit and play, right?" He waited until Jason
nodded, seeing Dave, Kipper and Michael were already busying
themselves in preparation for their performance. "And if you're
not any better, I'll take over, okay?" He patted Jason's shoulder
when he nodded again, glad to have that out of the way,
knowing that Jason would not give in easily. You had to admire
the man's determination...

"I really don't think..." Georgie was silenced with one look. She
held her hands up in surrender, getting to her feet and stepping
away from him.

Christopher shared a knowing look with her, pulling Jason to his
feet. "You look like death warmed up."

Jason smiled, rubbing the back of his neck. "I was jittery this
morning, and I've been flying off the handle all day." He laughed
softly. "It's definitely viral. You know how I hate being ill." He
looked at Georgie, aware now that it was just the three of them.
"I don't do illness." He joked, glad when she smiled.

"Ready?" Vince strode towards them, indicating the stage.
"Where's..."

"All set up, on the stand, waiting for you. We insist you sit it out." Vince cut him off, knowing that Jason's mind was on that bloody saxophone. If ever a man needed love in his life, it was Jason; his instrument dedication bordered on scary.

"Thanks." He staggered as he took a few steps forward, leaning against the nearest wall to steady himself. Sitting had been fine, standing up had made his head spin again but it had settled, yet walking was difficult. "Don't." He waved them away as he was approached on both sides.

Chapter 22

The room took a long time to stop spinning. Slowly; hesitantly, he opened one eye. No bright lights. That was a good sign. That meant the worst hadn't happened ... He opened the other eye, taking in his surroundings - Christopher's spare room. He groaned.

"So! You're awake at last!" Christopher perched on the edge of the bed, staring at his sickly sibling. "I've called Hamish, he said not to worry about tomorrow either."

Tomorrow? Jason's face creased into a frown. But...

"Tomorrow is Friday, Jason. I'm not surprised you're confused, you were well out of it. I don't suppose you remember?"

Jason's frown deepened, and Christopher chuckled.

"I reassured Hamish you'd be back on your feet by Monday." He gauged his brother's blank expression. "I'm surprised you don't remember *anything*."

A rush of memories filtered through Jason's brain. The roar of applause as Miracle finished. How violently sick he'd been backstage. Michael had turned on Kipper then, blaming him for poisoning Jason. Kipper pinned Michael against the wall in a rage. Christopher leading him out, and into a taxi. He then remembered being violently sick again, on the way home, at the side of the road; and again once they'd arrived in Kensington. And several times during the night. He groaned.

"They fought over me?"

Christopher laughed, softly. "Trust you to remember the most interesting bit of the evening."

Jason too laughed, soon stopping as the pain from his cramped stomach muscles spasmed. It flashed into his chest too; a horrible acidic burning.

"I'll get you some fresh water." Christopher got up, taking the glass from the bedside table, not two inches from Jason's head. "I also hope you didn't mind me answering your phone."

"My phone?" Jason repeated, unsure of what he'd heard.

"The bloody thing wouldn't stop ringing." Christopher said in his defence. "I turned it off in the end, when I figured out how." He chuckled softly, dropping it into Jason's lap.

"Who called?"

"Every man and his bloody dog!" Christopher hooted. "I only spoke to Georgie." He saw the horror cross Jason's face. "I said you were resting, you'd take a few days off and be right as rain by Monday."

Jason groaned.

It was Christopher's turn to frown. "I thought you'd want her to know."

"It's not that." Jason closed his eyes.

"Okay, well, save it. I'll be back in a minute." And with that, he left Jason to his thoughts.

Jason awoke in a cold sweat, sitting up far too fast and making his head thump. He could hear their raised voices; Kipper and

WHEN THE SAX MAN PLAYS PART 1 MAKING IT

Michael, Dave and Vince, with Georgie shrieking at all of them, unsure what was then and what was now. He drew his knees up to his chest, sinking his head in his hands. He looked up as Christopher put his head round the door.

"You've got a guest, are you free?"

"Who is it?" He muttered through clenched teeth.

"Gorgeous brunette, 5 foot 6, blue eyes, wearing a halo of concern." Christopher grinned at him. "Who the hell do you think it is?" He took in Jason's silence. "Either you're still delirious, or there's something you're not telling me about."

"What?" Weakness tautened his already soft voice.

"Georgie. Can I show her in, or do I have to fob the poor girl off?" He chuckled. "She's tracked you down this far, the least you can do is see her."

"Uhh... no." Jason turned another shade of grey; Christopher read the signs for what they were, pulling him to his feet and getting him into the bathroom, just in time.

Having made him promise that he would be alright alone for a while some ten minutes later, he retraced his steps back down the hallway, taking in Georgie's equally pale face.

"He sounds awful." Her eyes searched his face meaningfully. "Are you sure this is the best place for him?" She paused, taking in his surfacing anger. "I'm sorry, I know you know what you're doing. I just..." She took a deep breath, and he could see she was battling back tears.

"He's alright, honest. I wouldn't let anything happen to him. If I thought it was necessary, I'd do it. He's fine. It's a stomach bug, he's feeling very raw as you would expect."

Georgie nodded, knowing Christopher was right in everything that he said. "You're sure it's a bug?"

"Pretty certain." He watched as she breathed a sigh of relief. "Even if it wasn't, he's been so violently sick there's nothing left to do him any harm."

She pulled a face and he apologised. "Can I see him?"

My God! This girl is seriously in love! The thought flashed across his mind.

"I don't think that's a good idea." Christopher's attention halved as the floorboards creaked, tracing Jason's journey back to bed.

Georgie sighed reluctantly.

"I'll just check up on him." He got to his feet as she nodded. Indeed Jason was back in bed, one arm shielding his eyes, the cover half over him as he shivered.

"You are delirious, aren't you?"

"'m fine," Jason mumbled, barely aware of his presence.

"Yeah?" Christopher paused. "How many fingers am I holding up?"

Jason hadn't even bothered to look. "Go away." He mumbled.

"That's a nice thing to say to your brother who's looking after you."

But Jason was already asleep.

"You can peer in, if you must." Christopher strode back into the room, making her jump. "I wouldn't advise getting any closer - his temperature's 103, and he still looks like death warmed up."

Georgie looked at him, horrified. "I hope you don't get it too." She said, walking down the hallway with him.

Christopher shrugged. "I'm sure I'll be fine."

Jason blinked, rereading the message from Georgie.

REALLY WORRIED ABOUT YOU. LOOKED IN ON YOU. WILL COME BACK WHEN UR BETR - CHRIS RECKONS 2MRW. G XXX

She'd been here? Looking in on him? He groaned again, for a different reason. Having not eaten for the last 24 hours, suddenly he felt ravenous.

He read her words again. No-one got away with shortening his brother's name; hardly ever him, never mind a complete stranger... Not that she was a stranger. It had been nice when she was near. He'd enjoyed her touch - her arm around his waist; the rhythmic rubbing of his back, soothing him.

He sighed, swinging the duvet to one side, tentatively sitting up and risking putting his feet on the floor. Relief flooded through him when the walls stayed solid and the floor did not buck. Good. Normality!

Carefully, he got to his feet - still fine, no problem. His eye landed on the blue dressing gown on the chair nearest him, and he tugged it around him, taking careful then confident steps out to find Christopher - and raid the fridge.

"I'll leave you in peace." Christopher threw him a wink as he shut the door over, having escorted Georgie inside, relieving her of her coat before she sat down opposite Jason.

Jason was still staring incredulous at the closed door, having never seen Christopher wink before, nor give him that teasing look. He shook his head in disbelief, tuning his attention to his guest. He was surprised that she hadn't spoken yet, and blushed to see that she was looking at him intensely, instinctively drawing the dressing gown closer around him.

"I can't...."

"It's so..."

They both spoke at once, both stopping and smiling.

"After you."

Georgie shook his head. "No, after you." She felt the relief course through her, seeing the usual twinkle in his eye. He remained silent, so she plunged in. How was he? What did he remember? How did he feel now? Everyone had been asking after him, and she told him that she could only reply with a shrug of her shoulders. She told him how Hamish had called her into his office to ask about him, having heard she had contacted his brother.

Jason winced. Theirs was not a secret anymore then?

Georgie laughed, and Jason too smiled, the sound cheering him immensely. "I told him it was just friendly concern." She paused, taking in Jason's expression. "He just laughed, and winked at me as I left."

Jason groaned, putting his head in his hands. He was due for a surprise visit to Hamish's office on Monday, he could tell.

"But don't worry." Georgie walked across the room to sit next to him, putting her arm around him. "It's okay, because I've sat my final exams."

"Already?" He looked up, smiling to find her so close.

Georgie nodded. "You knew that was the plan."

He shifted, taking her hands in his. "I just hope it goes okay, so much is weighing on those grades."

Georgie rolled her eyes. "I was as ready as I would ever be. I sailed through it, there was only one tough section that required a bit more thought." She smiled at him. "It's fine, I know it is."

"Thank goodness!" He squeezed her hands, his smile widening when she squeezed him back.

Georgie laughed at herself. "It stopped me worrying about you."

"Aww! You sop!" Jason teased, hugging her. "There was no need to worry."

Georgie shook her head, feeling her hidden tears spill down her cheeks. "You collapsed! You've been so ill, Jas." She sniffed. "I wanted to look after you, to make sure you were okay." Her voice trailed to a halt.

"I'm a lucky man." He gave her a squeeze. "Two kind people with my best interest at heart." He shook his head in disbelief, knowing a change in conversation was required. "Christopher was impressed you tracked me down!" He joked.

"It took a while." She admitted, torn between her conflicting emotions - to pull away but look him in the eye, or to snuggle further into him, revelling in the feeling of being safe, in love, and wanted. She wiped her eyes with the back of her hand. "I went to your flat. Rang and rang the bell; called your phone several times. I gave in after ten minutes of trying to get an answer - and then as I sat on the step, totally lost, Christopher called me back."

Jason raised one eyebrow - *did he now? The sly devil!*

"He gave me directions but told me you were pretty rough."

Jason laughed. "Understatement of the century!"

Georgie too laughed. There and then a thought struck her: she had promised the guys she'd report back. She pulled her phone from her bag. "I'd better tell the guys you'll live."

"Wait a minute."

She looked fearfully at him.

"I mean, I'm fine. Remember, our first gig - on Sunday?"

"You can't possibly go!" Georgie gasped.

Jason nodded, but soon stopped, as it felt like his head would fall off with the motion. He rubbed his tense neck. "It'll be fine, we're looking forward to it, it'll be a great boost." He stopped, two thoughts striking him at the same time. He moaned. His eyes shot to her face. "What happened?"

"When?" Georgie frowned, confused.

"The contest." He massaged at the pain in his temples, letting go of her hands.

"Don't worry, we're through; we're both through." Mentally she kicked herself, waiting for him to exhale and worrying when he didn't... Suddenly she realised why. "And we had Fred open the store room in your section..." Jason's brain whirled: Fred... ah yes, Impervious' janitor. "...and safely lock away the sax." Then came the exhalation. Georgie almost smiled.

Georgie read the message early the next morning, surprised to see who it was from.

BACK HOME BUT CONFINED TO THE SOFA. PLS SAVE ME FROM BOREDOM! LOVE BEING WITH YOU. BRING DVDS AND FAVOURITE FOOD PLS. XXX

She laughed aloud, then frowned - what was his favourite?

"What're you laughing at?" Sophie smiled at her, being the first unusually to meet her in the park.

"Just a text."

"Oh yes?" Sophie raised an eyebrow inquisitively. "Anyone we know?" Georgie blushed, and Sophie shrieked. "You're shagging him?!"

"Don't be silly!" Georgie hissed. "And keep your voice down!" She looked around, but no-one else seemed to be interested in their conversation.

"Who's she shagging?" Leanne plonked herself down on the rug between the two.

Anna rolled her eyes, sitting down as gracefully as possible on the edge of picnic blanket. "Who do you think she's talking about?" She looked meaningfully at Leanne.

"Oh My God!" Leanne gasped.

"I'm not shagging him." Georgie hissed.

"Why the hell not?" Sophie leered.

Georgie shook her head.

"What's stopping you? You're a free woman, you've done all your exams so that means you don't jeopardise anything between you." Leanne offered, trying to think inside Georgie's head.

She was met with a nod. "Yes, but c'mon. You saw him, he's really ill."

Anna frowned. "He's not better yet?"

"Much, but not entirely." She pulled a face. "I've never heard anyone be so sick." She shuddered.

"A modern-day Florence Nightingale, eh?" Sophie nudged Leanne and they both laughed.

Georgie and Anna shared an unimpressed look, smiling at each other. Of the four, they shared the deepest bond. Sophie and Leanne complimented them, but they just... Georgie couldn't quite put her finger on it. She knew if she had any worries, she'd turn to Anna. Carefully, she stored the idea for future use, glad when Anna jumped to feet, proclaiming it was shopping time.

WHEN THE SAX MAN PLAYS PART 1 MAKING IT

Jason laughed as he let her in, relieving her of one of the many bulging bags she was struggling up the steps with.

"I'm so glad to see you. I'm sorry, I don't have anything that's remotely edible." He shuddered.

"That's okay, you have a valid excuse." Georgie kissed his nearest cheek as she walked past him and down the hallway, glancing out of the corner of her eye as he closed the door, leaning back on it. She smiled to herself. "I didn't know what you meant when you said favourite." She began, tipping a bag upside down on the kitchen work surface. "I bought half the shop." She giggled, displaying a carton of milk, fresh eggs and a freshly baked loaf (from that afternoon, but still tantalisingly fresh enough to make Jason's mouth water); tea bags and a jar of coffee; tins of soup and baked beans.

"You can tell you're a student, y'know." He teased.

Georgie spun round, playfully trying to punch him for that comment. She giggled as he grabbed her outstretched hands, pulling her towards him to hold her close.

His eye fell on the rest of the bags. "What else have you got?" Georgie squeezed him laughing. "All manner of interesting things. And if you're good, you'll get to see." She looked up when he didn't reply, laughing to see that he was play-pouting.

She looked across at him, seeing he was fast asleep not twenty minutes into the movie. It was only natural that he'd be wiped out after the last 48 hours. She had been silly to let the girls encourage her to add scented candles and sexy underwear to her purchases. But it wouldn't be wasted; they would consummate their relationship at some point, as yet she didn't know when, but she promised herself that she'd be ready.

She stretched, gently stroking her fingers down his face, tracing the stubble trail across his chin and cheeks, liking how the prickly sensation felt against her soft skin. That act itself was almost erotic, she giggled to herself, not wanting to wake him.

She leant over, wanting to kiss him, overbalancing and falling on top of him, jolting him from his sleep. They laughed, and he kept her close, wrapping her in his arms, stretching out on the sofa.

She fell in love with being this close to him, her senses filled with him. She swore if she listened hard enough she could hear his heart beating, and to her, that was the most romantic thing she'd ever experienced. They could stay like this all night, as far as she was concerned.

"I'm sorry," he mumbled, "I didn't mean to fall asleep on you."

"It's okay." She snuggled closer to him, re-securing her grip on him. "You're wiped out, it's not your fault."

Jason dropped a kiss on the top of her head, and Georgie nearly melted. "I'm not exactly great company, am I?" He laughed. "I invite you round, though I have no food and no entertainment - and then I fall asleep!"

"It's enough just being here." Georgie said softly, squeezing her eyes tightly closed, savouring the intimacy of their togetherness, almost as if she expected it to be taken away at any moment.

WHEN THE SAX MAN PLAYS PART 1 MAKING IT

"If you're sure." Jason whispered, smiling as he kissed her again. "It's not exactly courting you like a gentleman would for a lady."

It was Georgie's turn to laugh. "There's plenty time for that."

Chapter 23

He awoke, slowly, hardly daring to peer at the time; groaning when he saw it was barely eight o'clock. Sunday mornings were meant for lie-ins he'd always insisted; Christopher knew not to call him before noon on any given Sunday.

He sighed, turning over, nearly jumping out of his skin to find Georgie in bed with him. He looked around wildly for some sort of clue; something to jog his memory. But nothing. He peeked under the duvet - she was wearing one of his t-shirts, and she looked rather cute, if he didn't say so himself... That meant she hadn't intended staying.

Okay. He took a deep breath, watching her face for any signs of her wakening. None. Good. He wanted to sort out his head before she woke up - he needed to know what had happened. He didn't remember!

Staring at the ceiling, Jason's mind whirled. She had arrived armed with shopping, he'd fallen asleep as she put the first DVD on. *Right.* He'd woken up, yes, and apologised for falling asleep on her.

His brow furrowed in concentration. It could be innocent; perhaps he was reading more into the situation than was strictly necessary. He almost laughed at himself.

Carefully he folded back the duvet, keeping her warm, listening for a change in the steady rhythm of her breathing. Nothing. Good. He got up, slowly, praying that a spring would not creak as he tiptoed out of the room. Only then, he noticed he was wearing pyjamas.

Pyjamas?! He almost spluttered aloud. He never wore pyjamas! Georgie stirred and he fled before she woke properly.

Absently he stirred his coffee, sure it was too early for breakfast, despite the shock to his system. He'd hurriedly washed and dressed in the bathroom, bolting for the kitchen, taking comfort from a mug of strong coffee. He jumped as Georgie's shadow fell over him.

"Sorry." She smiled her apology, sitting on the stool opposite him. "Are you okay?"

One glance told him that she too was dressed, and for some bizarre reason he felt reassured by this. "I'm fine," he swallowed hard, "how're you? How did you sleep?" He enquired politely.

"Like a log." She smiled at him, trying to read his expression. "You don't remember much about last night, do you?" She laughed as he looked up at her, amazed by her insight.

"No." He laughed, nervously running his hand through his hair.

"Don't worry, I didn't expect you to." She reached across the table, peeling his hand from the mug and interlocking her fingers with his. "So," she paused, a mischievous look crossing her face. "I bet you have no idea how you got into bed."

Jason shook his head. "Into bed and in *pyjamas*." He stressed the word, to Georgie's confusion.

"Normal people wear *pyjamas*." She too stressed the word

unsure of what the problem was, letting go of his hand.

"I'm not normal." Jason's voice dropped an octave, but a hint of laughter resided there.

"Oh! Here was me thinking I was doing the right thing! Sorry!" Jason too laughed, before the awkwardness of the conversation flowed back into his mind. "Is this what you do at weekends - stay overnight with handsome men and strip them off when they fall asleep?" There was a half-teasing tone to his voice, she was sure.

"Only the invalids," she teased in reply, "I let the drunks sleep." Jason's eyes widened in horror, a second before he realised she was teasing him, then he laughed again.

"I'm sorry." Georgie's tone became more sombre. "I didn't think you'd be offended."

"I'm not offended."

"Upset then." Georgie crossed her arms in front of her chest, ignoring the rumbling from her empty stomach. This was not how she imagined their first breakfast together would be. She felt a lump rise in her throat.

Jason shook his head. "I'm not, please Georgie, don't get me wrong." He let out a long, slow sigh, contemplating the silence between them and what it meant. "It was a complete shock to me." He blushed. "I've never woken up beside someone before."

Georgie's eyes widened in shock. "But..."

"But what? Surely I've had girlfriends?"

WHEN THE SAX MAN PLAYS PART 1 MAKING IT

"Well...." Georgie chewed her lip nervously. "Yes."

Jason shrugged. He'd imagined having this conversation with her, but not quite like this.

Georgie descended into hysterical laughter, tears trickling down her face. "This is where you say you're... gay, right?" She stood up quickly. "Why didn't you..."

"Stop." Jason shook his head, moving towards her. "You're wrong. I don't know where you got that idea from - you know I'm crazy about you, Georgie." He wrapped her quivering body in his arms, holding her in tightly. He kissed her head, squeezing her. "I'm in love with you, Georgie. No-one else." He took a deep shaky breath. "Please listen to me. It's been awkward between us, the whole student and tutor thing, but that's over now. You understand why we had to wait, don't you? I thought you understood, but maybe not." He squeezed his eyes closed, wondering how he'd managed to make such a mess of it all...

"No." Georgie sniffed, squeezing him so tightly it made him gasp. "I did understand - I resented it, but I understood. I didn't want to be the cause of you losing your job. I knew 'us' would result in that."

Jason breathed a sigh of relief. "So where did that come from?"

"You..." she sniffed. "Why were you so..." She trailed off. "You really don't remember what happened last night?"

Jason shook his head, still clasping her tightly.

"So I could tell you we made love until the small hours?" She began to laugh, seeing how farcical the whole situation was.

"Surely I would remember that...!" Jason too laughed. "I guess it's a boring story - I fell asleep on you, you being the sensible girl you are tried waking me but I didn't, so you got me into bed, somehow, deciding it was best to get me into pyjamas. Then you got in with me as it was getting late and you too were tired, thus you fell asleep with me."

Georgie nodded, trying not to laugh again. "Something like that." She pulled away from him, looking into his eyes, smiling when he did. "Next time I'll leave you crumpled on the sofa!"

Jason laughed again, bringing her in close, holding her against his chest, kissing her hair. "Thank you." He nuzzled into her neck, kissing her. "I don't know what I did to deserve you, you're far too good for me."

"Perhaps." Georgie kissed him back. "But maybe not." She pulled away from his embrace, sitting down again at the breakfast bar. "How about breakfast, or do you starve your guests?"

Jason laughed again. "I'm not usually up 'til ten-thirty at the earliest!" He paused. "I have a boring breakfast - Weetabix and grapefruit, and strong coffee, I'm sure you..."

"Sounds great." Georgie cut him off, leaning back in the chair. "Begin when you're ready." She joked, watching his expression turn from disbelief to relief as he smiled. "Two sugars please." She added, when he didn't move after a few minutes.

"Slave driver." He teased, leaning over to kiss her before collecting whatever was necessary - bowls, spoons, another mug, milk, box of cereal and jar of coffee, clicking on the kettle once more.

The hours flew by until he realised it was almost time to get ready for their performance at Fats. He insisted on escorting Georgie home that afternoon, despite the fact that he then had to reverse the whole journey to get himself ready.

Panic seized him as he realised he'd be performing without a saxophone. He clicked onto Glenn's number in his phone, thanking him countless times as he promised him a loan of his own heirloom. As the train slid into Hammersmith station, Jason alighted with the usual spring in his step.

He hurried through his wardrobe, overruling his first, second, third and fourth choices before settling on the first outfit. Jason chuckled to himself, unsure of why he couldn't make a simple decision. Was love the culprit?

"Hey stranger, how're you feeling?" Sabrina smiled, sitting beside him.

Jason looked at her blankly.

"Did you hit your head too?" She joked, glad when he smiled. "I've never seen someone faint so dramatically!" She laughed.

"What's dramatic about crumpling like paper?" Jason teased, finding his voice. He took in her outfit, concluding she was going out for the evening, wondering if she was meeting her boyfriend.

"No Jason, you didn't crumple, you went rigid." She slapped

her palms together. "Out like a light. Caused quite a stir."
Jason groaned, hiding his head in his hands. Sabrina chuckled,
and he realised that he liked that sound.

She touched his arm, and he looked up at her, seeing her green
eyes search his face. Teasingly she licked her lips, and Jason's
attention was locked onto her mouth, imagining what it would be
like to kiss those lips...

He shook himself. What was he doing? He had Georgie, and
he was happy with her. Wasn't he?

Chapter 24

Georgie stopped, causing Leanne, Sophie and Anna to also halt.

"What's wrong?" Anna retraced her steps, linking her arm with Georgie's. Her gaze followed Georgie's, and then she saw Jason and Sabrina. Sabrina was laughing madly at something he'd said, and he was wearing that megawatt grin. "Now..." she began.

"That bastard!" Sophie exclaimed, cutting her off.

"What the *fuck* is he playing at?" Leanne virtually hollered.

All four had been wrapped up in how the weekend had been portrayed, though the trio were disappointed nothing physical had happened, and they were in a self-congratulatory mood.

"Girls!" Anna raised her voice. "It might be innocent." She paused, taking in how her friends were looking at her. "Maybe she's just someone he knows."

Georgie half-nodded, still dazed.

"You look gorgeous Georgie, if you'll permit me to say so." Christopher smiled, meeting them at the entrance to Fats.

She torn her eyes from the couple to look at him, tears stinging the back of her eyes, trying to believe Anna's words.

"What's wrong?" He took a few steps towards her.

Georgie realised then that the girls were quiet; bowled over by Christopher's towering frame.

"Jason's brother, Christopher." She managed through clenched teeth, taking a deep breath.

"Who's the broad?" Leanne indicated over her shoulder at

WHEN THE SAX MAN PLAYS PART 1 MAKING IT

Jason and his partner.

Christopher looked, frowning. "I've never seen her before."

Anna shared a triumphant glance around her.

"She's a stunner, isn't she?" Christopher's observation slipped out of his mouth before he could stop it.

The four around him gasped, and then he realised his mistake: he put two and two together.

"No, no," he shook his head, "it's not what you're thinking - Jason's mad on Georgie. I'm sure the woman's just a friend. There's no need to worry." He put his arm around Georgie, steering her inside, her friends following. "C'mon, we need a drink to settle a few nerves." He squeezed her, glad that she was regrouping. "My round, I insist." He winked at the three following in his wake, wondering about the mystery woman that Jason seemed so comfortable around; understanding Georgie's shock.

He met Jason's eye from across the room, making a 'come here' gesture that Jason knew better than to ignore. Sabrina followed him, taking in the atmosphere, having never before been in a jazz club. Indeed it was a new feeling for most people there to cheer on Impervious' groups.

"Introduce me to you lovely lady friend." He said, raising his glass to Sabrina. Once introduced, he leant towards Jason so that he was speaking out of Sabrina's earshot. "Georgie thinks she's been replaced." He nodded at Sabrina.

Colour drained from Jason's face, and Christopher nodded to

himself, glad that his theory had been proved. Jason rushed off to search for Georgie, leaving Sabrina with Christopher, who shrugged and asked her what she would like to drink?

Jason remained in a congratulatory mood from last night's performances. Both bands received an enormous amount of praise and flattery from the members of Fats; even Glenn himself. So much so, he had invited them back as regulars.

The significance of this stood out in Jason's mind. By then the competition winner would be known, and set to recording no doubt...

He dared not let his mind dwell on the thought. No. He had to focus. He had students to tutor; and the bands to perform with - and a great girlfriend to boot. The smile spread across his face just thinking about her... He didn't hear the door opening, but he soon saw the two masked men enter the room.

"Just another bloody inner City crime." Christopher shook his head. He of all people knew there was no justice in the world, one look at his patients told you that, but still, it was just a statistic until it happened to you. Once was unbelievable; twice was suspicious. He hoped that CCTV images from Impervious' cameras would ensure the culprits were brought to justice.

Time dragged by so slowly, as it does when on bedside vigil. He got to his feet, sighing. His finger on his phone hovered over the 'call' button; he was used to making life-changing phone calls, so what was the problem?

Heading outside once more, he summoned his courage to ring
Georgie's phone, half-hoping she wouldn't answer. She did. Her
expression sombred when she saw his pale, concerned face. Her
gut spasmed, knowing that he would not call her unless....

"They had a break-in at Impervious." He took a deep breath.
"My idiot brother stood up to them." His voice cracked.
Georgie swallowed hard, seeing the pain etched into his face.
"Is..." She couldn't bring herself to finish the sentence. "Where
are you? I'll come." She paused, wracking her brain for the
nearest hospital to Impervious. "Chelsea and Westminster?" She
guessed, relieved when he nodded, as this meant only a twenty
minute journey from where she was. "He's not..." She tried to
choke back the lump in her throat.

"He hasn't woken up yet." He gave her a small smile. "It would
be nice to have you here."
Despite herself, Georgie felt touched by this admittance - and
relieved by his choice of words.

"I'll meet you in the lobby." Christopher ended the call when
she agreed, casting his eyes heavenwards, toying with his
contrasting emotions - did he make another call, or didn't he?

They sat in silence, occasionally looking at the other, yet without
locking eyes.

"What about your parents, do they know?" Georgie said
suddenly, looking intently at him.

198

WHEN THE SAX MAN PLAYS PART 1 MAKING IT

Christopher raised one eyebrow. It was almost as if she'd read his mind: he'd been feeling guilty about not to calling them.

"I know they don't speak, but Jas always makes the effort." She paused. "I'd want my parents to know if anything happened to me, not necessarily to have them here but just so they knew." Christopher realised she was right; nodding and getting to his feet again. Georgie couldn't help but smile, glad he was the reliable type. He'd filled her in on what little he knew on the way through the twisting corridors, telling her Jason had woken up between then and now, and was sleeping it off while the test results were being analysed. The violent blow across his head had needed ten stitches; the rest of him was literally black and blue bruising.

It struck her, sitting here, the contrast between his pale skin and the bright flame-red colouring of his hair. She came out of her thought-induced trance, realising he was moaning - in pain.

"Jas?" She shuffled closer to him, taking his nearest hand in hers. "Jas, it's alright, sshh." She gave a little squeeze on his fingers, not daring to touch him in fear of causing him more pain.

Daytime was mixing with drug-induced dreaming, Jason realised, as the bright light got brighter, and the pain became more real. Alarm bells rang relentlessly in his mind; for a moment, he was unsure whether they were real or not. They were from the alarm warning system at Impervious, in a flash he traced it. He shuddered, triggered sharp stabs of pain. Stabs. Did they have knives? They each had a crowbar. A gun?

WHEN THE SAX MAN PLAYS PART 1 MAKING IT

Confusion wrestled his mind.

They'd hit him, more than once, he felt the red-hot burning pain slice through his head. That was then and that was now. His chest tightened as the pain increased, another bolt coming from that area... his stomach, his chest, he wasn't sure which.

"Jason, let the drugs work." Christopher's voice came to him, breaking through, pulling him to the surface of reality.

"...my head..." Even his own voice sounded strange.

"We know, they're giving you another shot now."

Jason winced as the syringe scratched his arm.

"You poor soul." Georgie whispered, leaning over him after the nurse had retreated. "You'll be okay, Jas."

"Georgie?" His voice, though thick with sleep, was confused.

"I'm here, don't worry, we're going to look after you." She squeezed his hand, smiling when he squeezed back.

"Get some sleep Jason, I mean it, let the drugs work." Christopher was on his other side he realised, his hand resting on Jason's shoulder protectively.

They both drifted into faint background.

Yet again Christopher insisted on having Jason stay with him in Kensington. Georgie was relieved that he cared so much, unable to imagine that their parents didn't. She had asked what their response to the news had been, but Christopher had shrugged, and she knew better than to pry. She made the journey across London with them when they released Jason, and was *very* surprised when Christopher said she could stay with them if she wanted to. She studied his face for a hidden meaning.

"I thought it was getting too late to be travelling." He added, as if he felt she needed an explanation.

Georgie hesitated, knowing there would be no problem with her parents. She had been raised to be honest at all times, and she had been - she decided she would call them to relay the plan.

Initially, they were not best pleased that Georgie had chosen now to start a relationship, especially as Jason was a tutor at Impervious - but after much arguing, they'd come to a truce.

She didn't know why Christopher was making this offer - it was eight o'clock, it wasn't that late. Did he have an ulterior motive? She knew he was reliable and trusted him, sure that she would be safe if she did stay.

"Don't let me pressure you." He smiled at her kindly.

"I know you're not." She smiled back at him. "Do you want me to stay?"

"I wouldn't mind." He paused. "And no, I'm not going to steal my brother's girlfriend either." He teased. "I have far too much respect for you. An aspiring lawyer indeed! I may require your services at some point, so I need to keep on your good side - besides, one day you will be my sister-in-law."

Shock was written plainly across Georgie's face. She was clearly clueless: Christopher found this amusing.

"Put the pieces together. He's never had a proper girlfriend. He doesn't stop talking about you. You're equally as besotted as he is." He shrugged. "Why not? It's perfectly logical."

Georgie let out her breath slowly, trying to take all this in - a difficult task while her mind was doing cartwheels. "I'll just make a phone call, if you don't mind." She said, taking her phone from her bag, trying to keep her voice normal.

"Sure. I've got the kettle on, would you like something? Tea?"

"Tea would be fine, thank you, milk and two."

Christopher nodded, disappearing into the kitchen to give her privacy, wondering who she was calling... He made as much noise as he could, letting her know that he wasn't listening, clanging spoons on the mugs and humming to himself, unsure quite how he was going to entertain his extra guest.

Anna looked at her phone in disbelief, rereading the message.

MUST MEET 2MRW - IMP. NEWS. STAYING WITH JAS 2NITE AT CHRIS'S, HE WAS BEATEN UP - 10 STITCHES! TALK SOON. G XXX

Her initial reaction was to text the others, but she wondered if this was a message just for her... She brought up the sender information, learning that it was not a group text. That alone spoke volumes. She decided to phone her back.

Georgie excused herself from the room when her phone began to ring.

"What's going on?" Anna greeted her.

"It's a long story," Georgie warned her.

"Start speaking girl, I can't wait 24 hours!"

Georgie grinned. "Where do you want me to start?"

"What happened to Jason?"

"He was beaten up..."

"This morning?"

Georgie nodded. "They broke into Impervious,"

"No!" Anna gasped, cutting her off. "Past security?"

Georgie nodded sorrowfully. "I don't know how. They sought him out, they could've killed him." A tremor rippled in her voice.

"Ten stitches is a hell of a lot." Anna probed, sensing her friend was starting to drift with her sad thoughts.

Georgie nodded. "A crowbar."

"Fuckin' hell!" Anna swore. "I'm surprised it didn't kill him."

Georgie nodded again. "The doctor told us he was lucky, an inch either way and it might've been a different story."

"Bastards!" Anna shook her head, deciding to change the subject. "What's the important news?"

"I'm going to be the future Mrs Bottelli." Georgie spoke slowly, testing out the name.

"WHAT?!" Anna spat.

WHEN THE SAX MAN PLAYS PART 1 MAKING IT
Chapter 25

This is what they wanted! Jason could scream in frustration.

Hamish had insisted on having him signed off work for the week, which impinged on the Semi-finals of the competition, telling him that under no circumstances was he to participate.

Jason's heart sank: Miracle were not as polished without him, obviously, and their ranking would suffer because of this. Deep down, he knew it was a blessing to be given a reprieve, unsure of whether he could cope with the rigours of stage performance.

The band members had taken this news very well, despite the circumstances, with everyone agreeing they would meet up in a week. Jason promised to be there on the night to support them. Vince then called and told him he was standing in as his replacement with Georgie's Guys and for a split second, Jason wondered if Dave had confided in him, but he trusted the youngster to keep his word. Perhaps this was just Vince's way - stepping up in times of need. Jason thanked him profusely, trying to reassure him that he would heal and he was being looked after. Vince had laughed then, telling him that he had great taste.

This threw Jason completely. Only after the call had ended, he realised what Vince was implying: everyone knew about his relationship with Georgie. That discussion with Hamish was now overdue. But Hamish, for his part, was the concerned employer. Christopher pointed out that he was probably only placating Jason in case he wanted to sue the College. This only confused

WHEN THE SAX MAN PLAYS PART 1 MAKING IT

Jason further...

Tuesday evening rolled around and he decided it would be best to return to his own flat the next day. He hated feeling like he was encroaching on someone else's life, especially Christopher's: his brother had a stressful, busy job and the last thing he needed was to come home and start all over again.

Christopher shrugged. He didn't mind either way, but whatever made Jason feel better, just as long as he felt safe. Safe? The frown creased Jason's face as a series of horrifying images reeled across his mind.

Christopher winced, wishing he hadn't opened his mouth. "Why don't you stay a little longer? You can invite whoever you like round, I don't mind."

"You don't like the idea of me being alone, do you?" Jason's voice was a whisper.

"Not after what happened. I needed to know you truly were okay." He didn't share what concerns the doctor had - one medical professional to another - deciding his brother suffered vivid enough nightmares as it was.

Georgie hugged him in tightly when she saw him the following day, suggesting they go out for lunch, sure that the fresh air would do them both good.

She had another week before she began at MacMillan's, and she still wasn't 100% sure that she actually wanted it. She'd confided this to her girlfriends: they all dismissed it for nerves, telling her she'd be fine; she'd always wanted this, reminding her how lucky she was to land such a well paid job straightaway. Georgie nodded absently, trying to believe what they said.

She looked across the table at Jason, who was looking around them a little wildly, his expression tense and nervous. She leant across the table to take his hands, making him jump. "What's wrong?"

"Nothing, it's okay." Jason closed his eyes and took a deep breath. "I'm just..." He swallowed hard. "...jumpy, I guess."

"Is it here?" Georgie too looked around them. "Do you want to go somewhere else?"

"I don't know." His panicked expression said everything. Georgie kicked herself for not seeing this coming. She had thought that just by being with her, as a distraction, it would make a difference.

"C'mon." She gave his hands another squeeze, getting to her feet. "We'll go somewhere else." She linked her arm through his, leading him outside, almost able to feel his relief as they stepped into the crisp city air. Poor Jason was shaking, as he had been that first night she'd spent with him.

Immediately she hugged him in tightly, squeezing him. "I'm sorry Jas, I didn't think..."

He cut her off with a shake of his head. "It was a good idea." He took a deep breath. "I just need to get a grip." He laughed at himself, but sadly, feeling her squeeze him again.

"Don't be silly, it's only natural." Gently she kissed him. He nodded silently, receiving another kiss, breathing in her scent - Gucci wasn't it? "Do you want to go back?" Georgie was trying to gauge his thoughts, but he hadn't moved in the last few minutes, at times she was unsure that he was still breathing.

"No." He shook his head again. "I need to get out. I need to get back to normal." He sighed. *How the hell was he going to cope returning to Impervious tomorrow night?*

Georgie made a very sweet gesture, travelling out to Kensington to meet them the next night, relieved they weren't travelling via the Tube network, sure that Jason would hate the attention that would be lavished upon him. It was human nature to stare at something that was horrifying, and his injuries were certainly that. Deep purple bruising covered his face, she knew too that his back, chest and arms were the same. He didn't voice his pain, but it was obvious that he felt it.

Christopher's car was, she felt, a typical doctor's car - a black BMW with cream leather seats. It was certainly a beast that spoke of the owner's wealth, shiny and new. She expected to sit in the back, watching over the two of them, surprised when Jason sat in the back beside her. Christopher shared a knowing glance with her in the rear-view mirror. Again she felt thankful that he was so supportive - the thought struck her that he was all Jason had. She shook her head with her thoughts.

"Are you sure about this?" Christopher turned round to face his passengers in the back.

Jason nodded. "Yes." He paused. "I need to return, I can't stay home forever." He sighed. "If there's a job for me, that is."

"Of course there is!" Christopher could see from Georgie's expression that she too was horrified by Jason's admittance. Carefully Jason shook his head, but they could see how upset he was. "I'm a laughing stock, nobody takes me seriously there, and they're hardly likely to now. What will I do if the bands fail?" He shook his head sorrowfully.

"We won't fail." Georgie was shocked by his words, exchanging a worried look with Christopher. "Vince has taken over, it's going to be fine. Worst cause scenario only one group go through, but you can't blame yourself. It wasn't your fault, Jas." She shuddered. "Those guys wanted rid of you, for some reason, and they achieved their aim, but we'll carry on. So what if you don't tutor a group who wins the competition? Big deal. You're a great tutor, with real talent. Who cares about the rest of them? You have Hamish's blessing and that's what counts; that's what keeps you at Impervious. Nobody else matters." She squeezed his hand, seeing his face fall further.

"But I want to win."

"We know." Christopher's voice was soft but firm. "Georgie's right - what the other tutors say means nothing. Just because you've had a few awkward situations doesn't mean you give up."

Jason battled the tears welling in his eyes. "So they try to kill me and I go back for more?"

Silence fell between them.

Georgie unclipped her seatbelt to shuffle across to hold him.

"Of course not. We don't mean it like that." Exasperation grated in Christopher's voice.

"I know." Jason hugged Georgie tighter, thankful for her presence. "I'm sorry, I didn't mean..." He breathed out slowly. "Let's go. I have to do this, and I can't do it without you two."

"If you're sure." Georgie kissed him before scooting back over to refasten her seat belt, nodding at Christopher, who was waiting for Jason to nod his confirmation.

"You lot should be in there." Jason waggled his finger teasingly at the small gathering congregated at the foot of the stairs. Just seeing them all brought a smile to his face.

"What for?" Kipper challenged. "We don't need to check out the competition, we already know we can beat them." He clapped Jason on the shoulder, making him wince before backing off and apologising.

"Are you okay, seriously?" Michael asked.

Dave and Vince nodded, wanting to ask the same question.

"I will be. Nothing the wonders of modern medicine can't cure." He gave them a half-smile, seeing their serious expressions and hating every minute of it. "Please, don't worry. I got off lightly."

"You shouldn't have fought back." Dave was shaking his head.

"I didn't have a choice." Jason shuddered, trying to ignore the reel of horrible images filtering through his mind. "We should go in, what time are we on?" He caught the group's hesitancy. "I mean you. I can't do anything like this." He regretted that last sentence, seeing their grave expressions return.

He gestured to Christopher to lead the way, damn sure he wasn't going to go in first, knowing that people would turn to look... The plan was to slip into the back row. At some point, he knew he would become centre of attention.

Hamish was waiting for them at the hall entrance: Jason groaned softly. And so the quizzing began: how was he? Where was he staying? Hopefully he was resting? If there was anything he could do, he was just to say. It was great to see him and would they like to sit in the front?

Inwardly, Jason swore. Walking down the many steps to the front of the auditorium, tiny fireworks of pain went off as the movements jarred his battered body. Hamish told him he wasn't to worry about not being able to perform; Miracle would not be punished because of his absence. And as for Georgie, she was a lovely girl and he wished them both the best. Jason cringed, wishing for a hole to appear and swallow him!

Christopher kicked into overprotective mode when Hamish left several minutes later, fending off anyone who arrived with best wishes and concerns.

Jason wondered why the hell he had come, his head throbbing from the combination of warm air, musical instruments warming up and unwanted attention...

WHEN THE SAX MAN PLAYS PART 1 MAKING IT

"I've got the eight o'clock slot, and Miracle have half-seven." Georgie sat beside him, laying her hand on his arm. "Everyone's asking after you, I told them all that you're fine."

It seemed silly to go along with Jason's ruse - that he was truly fine and on the way to recovery - when it seemed so obvious that he wasn't. However, nobody passed comment, so it was a ruse that was working. Only the three of them knew the truth.

As before, Hamish led the welcome ceremony. Jason winced as Hamish publicly wished him a speedy recovery, promising they would catch the culprits. He groaned.

"Ah, he had to." Christopher whispered. "How awful would it be for the Principal not to acknowledge the staff tutor?" He shook his head. "Poor man was cornered into that one."

Jason flinched, recalling he'd been backed into a corner... The two masked men had taken their time, drawing in on him; both armed. His chest and head throbbed accordingly with the memory. He swallowed hard, feeling the waves of panic crashing over him again.

Georgie had been watching him as Hamish took to the stage; watching his pale face turn grey. She put her nearest arm around him, taking his other hand with hers, talking calmly to him. Her own memories rolled around her mind: the first night she'd stayed with him in Kensington, how panicky he'd been then, and subsequent nights afterwards. She'd panicked herself, rushing out of the room to find Christopher, hating to leave him but knowing she had little choice. She'd never been in this situation before, and she didn't know what to do to calm him, but she knew Christopher would. She learnt fast.

"We should get some fresh air." She spoke softly, aware of more than a few sets of eyes on them.

"No." Jason spoke through gritted teeth. "I can't leave." This was made worse by the fact he would have the eyes of the room on him, following them. His knuckles turned white, and Georgie could feel him start to shake. She looked past him at Christopher.

"Sure we can, then we can slip into the back as things get going. The music's going to make your head thump more anyway." He gave her a small smile over Jason's head. "It's going to bring everything back, being here again. Nobody said it was going to be easy." He spoke more softly, squeezing Jason's arm. "C'mon." He nodded at Georgie, both of them getting to their feet together, taking Jason with them.

People streamed in and out of the hall constantly, glancing at the trio sitting on the low wall in the corner, muttering between themselves. Christopher did a good job of fending off the extra attention, leaving Georgie to reassure Jason.

"He's fine." Christopher said again, seeing yet another well-wisher appear. "Just give us a minute."

Georgie looked up, seeing Vince, glad that he was alone. She shook her head in reply to his silent question, seeing him frown. Jason had his head buried into her shoulder; she automatically rubbed his back, expecting but dreading him to sob.

"What can we do?" Vince spoke softly.

"Nothing." Georgie shook her head. "He needs to work it out of his system."

"I'd be scared shitless if it was me." Vince shook his head in sympathy.

"Please." Christopher held his hands up.

"Sorry." Vince shared another look with Georgie. "I'll give you peace." He hesitated, receiving two nods from the pair. "Jas, don't worry about us, okay? We're gonna bloody win this competition." He saw Georgie and Christopher smile, and hoped Jason was too. He gave them a nod, leaving them in peace as promised.

"We'll sit it out until seven-thirty." Christopher announced, consulting his watch. "Nobody will see us creep back in and we can leave again soon after." He smiled at Georgie. "Until you're on, that is. Then we'll creep away quietly for the night." He spotted Hamish heading towards them, standing up to head him off.

"You shouldn't have him here."

Christopher shrugged. "I tried, but he was adamant."

Hamish gave him a small smile. "That's a good sign."

Christopher too smiled. "I know, I thought the same myself." He frowned. "We've just got to get past the demons."

"Have you arranged counselling?"

Christopher shook his head. "It's too soon for that."

WHEN THE SAX MAN PLAYS PART 1 MAKING IT

Hamish's lips pursed in disagreement and Georgie could see Christopher was ready for an argument: folding his arms across his chest.

"He's too fragile. The brave face is all a front."

Hamish's nod said *I did wonder...* "As long as you're sure."

Christopher nodded. "Yes. We'll regroup and come back in."

Hamish gave Georgie a nod before heading back into the hall where the first group were warming up.

Jason was drowning in his panic, unable to think; unable to control himself. His chest tightened, increasing the pain from his multiple injuries, making his shallow breaths shallower still. Everything around him was blocked out; noise, lights, people. His grip around Georgie slackened.

"Jason!" She squeezed him, looking around them for Christopher, knowing what was happening. "Christopher!" She couldn't see him, and her own panic threatened to swamp her.

"It's alright." Christopher appeared, hovering by her elbow. "It's alright. Jason, listen to me, you've got to focus. Focus on the breaths, in, and out, in, and out, take it easy, you're alright. Stay with us, okay?" He took control, getting Jason to breathe with him, both of them reassuring him.

"I'm sorry," Jason whispered minutes later, keeping his head on Georgie's shoulder, revelling in the comfort of her touch.

"You can't help it, Jas." She said softly.

Jason shook his head, still feeling light-headed and sick.

"This wasn't a good idea." Christopher shook his head. "It's far too soon. You've got to have strength to put on a brave face. Strength you don't have yet."

To Georgie's horror, Jason broke down. "Hey!" She stared at Christopher, who shrugged. "It's not his fault." She blinked away her own tears, filling with disgust.

"You know what I mean."

"No, frankly I don't." She looked defiantly at him. "We don't know how he feels, so we can't judge."

Christopher threw his hands in the air and rolled his eyes. "So! You've been here five minutes and you know more about my own brother than I do?"

"Stop it, both of you." Jason took a few juddering breaths, sitting up straighter. "I'm sorry I ever took this bloody job!"

"No!" They both said together, both putting their arms around him.

"No Jas, don't say that." Upset resounded in Georgie's voice.

"You know that's not true." Christopher added.

Jason shook his head. Over the silence, the music drifted across and they got to their feet, recognising the piece. Silently they called a truce, sitting through both bands' performance before calling it a night.

Georgie lay wide awake in her own bed, listening to the silence. In the darkness, the glow from her phone turned her face a vibrant green as she reread the messages from each brother.

I SHOULDN'T HAVE BEEN SO SHORT WITH YOU, I KNOW YOU HAVE GOOD INTENTIONS. THANK YOU - FOR EVERYTHING. FORGIVE ME? CHRISTOPHER.

Georgie let her breath out slowly. Was it her fault? He was a sensitive soul, and he cared deeply about his brother, perhaps that was the reason behind his unusual temper?

THANX 4 2NITE, KNOW IT MUST'VE BEEN HARD. BED FEELS EMPTY WITHOUT YOU. CAN'T BE WITHOUT YOU. MISS YOU! CU 2MRW? J XXX

She took another deep breath, fighting her rising tears for the second time that night. Onstage and consumed with emotion, she'd almost forgotten her words. The auto cue rolled and she'd thought of Jason, immediately wanting to howl. Taking a few deep breaths and looking around at her fellow performers had given her that inner strength. Until then, she hadn't known it had existed.

Later, when Christopher stopped the car in her street, they'd exchanged no words as she'd slammed the car door shut, running up the steps and letting herself into her parent's house, heading straight to her room and throwing herself on the bed.

Her eye fell on the clock. 1:03 am. Jason's message had arrived five minutes ago. She fired off a quick reply and put the phone down, turning over. His reply arrived moments later.

I'M SO SORRY, GEORGIE. I FEEL RESPONSIBLE FOR THIS MESS. CALL ME WHEN YOU GET THIS, I NEED TO KNOW YOU'RE OK. MY HEAD'S TOO MUCH OF A MESS. CAN'T DEAL WITH GOING BACK. XXX

Georgie's resolve melted. Despite the time, it was obvious they were both awake. She called him, wishing she was there instead of at the end of the phone.

Jason dragged himself out of bed, feeling worse for his lie-in. He read his brother's note on the kitchen table, making his decision.

Christopher had admitted his misjudgements when Jason was thinking straight. To go through that and come out relatively unscathed he knew was damn near impossible; yet Georgie had managed it. True, Christopher's behaviour could be accounted for by his overprotective nature but if anything, Georgie was his equal. She too only had Jason's best interests at heart.

He sighed. Last night had been hell. Not only with the vivid, recurring nightmares but the emptiness of his life; the whole place felt empty, as if there was something missing. There was, of course, but some*one* not some*thing*.

He forced himself to eat a late breakfast, wondering what he was going to do until Christopher arrived home. It wasn't right to up and leave without saying thank-you and goodbye first.

Jason fidgeted through the day, unable to concentrate on anything; flicking through magazines and then TV channels. He would've done some tidying, or dusting, but it was already done. He dreaded to think what state his own place was in, having not been there for nearly a week. Turning his phone on, he smiled when it was inundated with messages from the band members.

HI JASON, MIRACLE TOOK 5TH; GG'S 6TH. HOPE UR FEELING BETR. SEE YOU SOON? VINCE.

HI! WE CAME 5TH & 6TH - 2B HONEST THAT WAS GOOD BUT YOU'LL BE BACK FOR THE FINAL. HOPE UR OKAY? MICHAEL.

J. WE'RE IN THE FINAL. RU BACK ON MON? K

HI JASON, HOPE UR OK? KNOW UR IN A LOT OF PAIN. WE'RE THINKING OF YOU. BOTH BANDS IN FINAL, AS YOU PROBABLY KNOW. TC. DAVE.

He wondered with what he would reply. Admittedly he felt

better this morning; a little stronger and able to think clearer. Work, however, was another kettle of fish. He headed out for a walk, feeling the need to clear his head.

Jason's phone bounced across the table as the message came through early on Monday morning. He smiled when he saw it was from Georgie, seeing she had reiterated what she'd said as she left last night.

He'd got up early, sending Georgie a good luck message on the train on the way in, arriving at Impervious an hour earlier than normal, determined to make it through the day.

Christopher had been supportive as usual; Georgie too, both telling him he didn't have to go back if he didn't feel ready yet. But he had made up his mind, and he was going. If he didn't, he dreaded ever taking the plunge again.

Summoning his courage, he got up to make himself another coffee. Catching his reflection in the window, he saw he still looked sallow (Christopher's word again). There was that usual twinkle in his eyes though, and that was good. He'd felt better, that was true, and who could blame him? But the inner turmoil couldn't be given a chance to thrive, or it would take over his entire life. He'd already beaten it once and now it was back for a second round...

Firstly, he would mark the huge pile of papers on his desk, which looked like student assignments from the last week, then he would see Hamish before the first lessons began. His first class was scheduled for 11 o'clock as normal, which gave him time to get his head round being in work again. The knock at the door made him jump. It was just before eight; there was little sign of life at Impervious this early.

"Who is it?" Jason's voice came out weakly as his throat dried. His heart was pounding in his chest. Suddenly, he was glad he had locked the door behind him as he'd come in earlier, though he felt incredibly stupid when he'd done it.

"It's me." Dave too sounded nervous, Jason realised as he sagged with relief.

As if thieves and muggers would actually knock! The thought struck him as he reached the door and flicked it open.

"I'm so glad to see you!" Dave smiled. "I had this horrible feeling you wouldn't come back." He stepped forward, hugging Jason, briefly. "You look better, how are you?"

"Getting there." Jason answered truthfully. "I haven't gone out of my mind yet."

Dave laughed with him at the joke, betting it wasn't far from the truth... "I'm glad." He smiled. "I'm going for breakfast, want to come with me?"

"Smithy's?" Jason smiled back at him, agreeing when Dave nodded, careful to re-lock the door behind them.

As the pair walked down the hallways and through the campus, they met one of the tutors - Chambers (Mathematics and Applied Physics) - who stopped and asked how he was, telling him that it was good to have him back. Jason only laughed when they were sitting down in front of Smithy.

"So." Dave shovelled another lot of bacon and beans into his mouth. "How long has this been going on between you and Georgie, you sly devil."

"Not long." Jason admitted, cutting another bacon sliver.

"Officially?"

"Not long." He repeated, giving Dave a smile.

"Aww, c'mon!" Dave laughed. "You can tell me."

"There were fireworks early on," Jason admitted, "but we made a pact to protect ourselves. I didn't want to distract her from her studies."

"You don't say." Dave teased.

Jason put down his cutlery, studying his counterpart's face. "I'm sitting with a changed man, aren't I?" He smiled when Dave did.

"Totally." Dave borrowed Kipper's favourite word. "Thanks to you. I've even got my own flat, well I'm sharing with Vince." He admitted.

"As good as." Jason shrugged, watching Dave nod.

"And I've decided what I want to do."

Jason frowned, and winced. "Do?" He repeated.

Dave was nodding ecstatically. "I'm going into teaching, like you." He laughed as Jason's face dropped in shock. "I've already been accepted. I start in September."

"Well done you!" Jason clapped him on the back.

"But don't worry," Dave paused as he scraped his plate clean.

"I still need your guidance."

Jason beamed at him. "You've got it. Anytime."

Kipper was pacing the Music block corridors as Jason warily turned the corner, half ready to run. "Where the hell have you been?" He wrung his hands exasperatedly. "I bloody *need* you and you're not here!"

"Calm down." Jason continued to walk towards him, noting his wild expression. "What's wrong?"

"I'll tell you what's fucking wrong - I'm getting kicked out!"

"Why?" Again Jason wanted to frown, but the stitches protested, winning the battle. "What have you done?"

"Maya's bloody Hamish's bloody niece!" Kipper spat.

It took Jason a second to remember who Maya was... His memory supplied him with the information - Kipper's pregnant ex-girlfriend. He unlocked the door, forgetting to cast a wary glance around the room, Kipper hot on his heels, spitting words at him at a-hundred-miles-an-hour.

"I need you to tell him I'm not as bad as he thinks!"

"Me?" Jason's eyes widened. "Why me?"

"He thinks the world of you! Don't you know?"

Jason shrugged. "What makes you think I'll change his mind?"

"It's worth a try!" Kipper paused, beginning to pace the room. "He won't listen to me! He keeps telling me to learn my lesson and do the right thing!"

Jason nodded, able to guess what the 'right thing' was. "Sounds like you're the one not listening." He said quietly.

"WHAT?!" Kipper thundered, striding towards Jason, his face black with anger.

"You can't wheedle your way out of things all your life." Jason spoke strongly, despite the fear he felt in the way Kipper was looking at him.

"What kinda *crap* is that?" Kipper leant over him menacingly.

"Back off." Jason spoke quietly.

His quiet tone shifted something in Kipper's brain. He sat down and apologised, an apology Jason waved away, relieved to have his own personal space again. Kipper apologised again, sinking his head into his hands.

Jason took a deep breath, trying to stop shaking. "Would it be so bad to do the right thing?"

Kipper's gaze rolled around the room before settling on Jason's face. "I...well, yeah, but..." He shook his head. "I don't know."

"What are you so scared of? All you can do is try."

Kipper nodded solemnly. "I'll think about it." He smiled at him, getting to his feet. "See you later?"

Jason nodded, feeling wiped out already, hardly daring to think that there were twelve hours between now and returning home.

"Jason?" Kipper put his head round the door, having nearly closed it. He waited until Jason looked up before speaking again. "Thanks." And with that, he was gone.

Jason let out his sigh of relief. And laughed.

WHEN THE SAX MAN PLAYS PART 1 MAKING IT

Georgie sighed into her phone at lunchtime. "I'm a just clerk."

Anna laughed. "What do you mean?"

"Make the tea, file, open the mail, answer the phone." Georgie pulled a face. "No real work."

Anna laughed harder, and Georgie frowned. "Georgie, you have to start somewhere! You can't just hop straight into a case." Anna paused. "What did you do on work experience?"

Georgie sighed, realising her friend was right; she smiled then. "You mean crawl before I can walk?"

Anna laughed again, and Georgie too laughed, wondering if her frustrations were getting the better of her? Anna had a point.

That afternoon she spent a few hours with one of the senior partners, Arnold, planning how her position would evolve. Her head was spinning by the time the clock chimed five.

Quickly, Georgie got her things together, said goodbye to her new colleagues and jumped on the first Tube to Impervious. Back to her other life, she smiled at the thought, realising that it wouldn't be for long: the Final was in less than two weeks!

As she walked towards the door, she could see that a new digi-lock had been installed. Two thoughts crossed her mind: it was good as it was an improved security measure, but she didn't know what the number was.

Fishing for her phone in her bag, she was unaware of the two men behind her. She jumped, heart hammering in her chest, spinning round so fast she almost fell over - it was Kipper and Dave! The relief made her laugh aloud.

Kipper gasped. "Georgie! You look SO sexy!" He took another step towards her, as if to paw her.

"Get off." She pushed him away playfully, laughing. "Or I'll get Jason onto you."

"Jason?" Kipper stopped walking, staring at her.

"You don't know?" Georgie looked to Dave, who shrugged.

"Know what?" Michael asked from behind them.

"I thought everyone knew!" Georgie frowned.

"Knew what?" Michael sensed he'd missed something.

"So did I." Dave shrugged when she looked at him, stepping forward to put the right code in, swinging the door open.

Kipper frowned. "Am I getting this right - you're shagging Jason?"

"What?!" Michael yelled.

"For God's sake!" Georgie groaned.

"But you are, aren't you?" Dave asked her, confused, still holding the door open.

"Not technically." Georgie blushed.

"But you're with him?" Dave tried to find the right words. Georgie nodded.

"C'mon you lot, I'm not holding this door open all night!" Dave shepherded them inside, ensuring the door locked behind them, all four walking the corridors together. "Well, I think it's great." He beamed at Georgie.

"Thank you." Georgie was still blushing.

Kipper was giving her a 'naughty' look but Michael looked quite upset. "Why didn't anyone tell me?" He wailed.

"I didn't know either." Kipper replied, looking at Dave. "How did *you* know?"

"It's obvious. She visited him in hospital, went to his brother's to see him, and came in with him on Thursday night. Haven't you seen the way his face lights up when she enters the room?"

Kipper shook his head. "Un-believ-able." He sucked his breath.

Michael shook his head, feeling like his world was caving in.

"Isn't it great?" Dave beamed at them.

"Great." Michael replied hollowly.

"Start." Jason waved his hands at the group. "I'll go'n see him."

Fifteen minutes later, Michael had still not appeared. Jason put two and two together when he heard that they'd all come in together and were talking about recent events when Michael decided to nip to the Gents before practice.

Shutting the door behind him, Jason swore. He knew this would happen: he'd known from day one. He was thankful that Michael was a strong character; sure that after a one-to-one, he could still get him to co-operate. Worst case scenario, he was one band down for the Final, and if he was honest with himself, that wouldn't necessarily be a bad thing...

Jason shook his head, this wasn't the time to think like that. He strode down the corridor, pushing open the correct door. One cubicle door was closed, so there were no prizes for guessing where Michael was.

WHEN THE SAX MAN PLAYS PART 1 MAKING IT

"There was going to be no easy way to tell you." Jason launched straight in. "It would've happened sooner or later." He leant against one of the sinks, feeling like he was talking to himself. "I'm flattered that you rate me this highly." He paused, waiting for a reply, of any sort.

"Why not?" Michael croaked. "You're wonderful."

Jason shook his head. "I'm not everyone's type of wonderful."

"You're my type of wonderful."

Jason cringed, glad that Michael couldn't see his reaction. "Thanks. It's good to know that I hold some sort of respect around here. You wouldn't think so with what's happened recently." He laughed bitterly.

Michael unbolted the cubicle door: it creaked violently as he opened it. "I knew you weren't gay." He spoke quietly. "But I hoped. Everyone's gotta hope, right?"

Jason smiled at him. "Are you here for the band, or for me?"

Michael toyed with his answer. "Both."

"Do you want to jack it all in?"

Michael was horrified by this idea. "No way! I love performing, and it's thanks to you I discovered my vocation." He beamed at Jason. "I'm going to the Royal College of Music next year." He said shyly.

"Good." Jason beamed back. "You only get one chance, and you should grab it with both hands."

"Is that what you did with Georgie?"

Jason just laughed.

There were eight finalists, he learnt - six groups and two duos. Jason rewound the tape from the Semis, studying the winners. In between performances, his mind wandered.

How was Vince faring? He'd heard from everyone else but him. He thought about Georgie too. She was on the other side of the city at MacMillan's, too far away to meet for lunch. Now they didn't have to hide their relationship, they naturally wanted to spend more time together. But how would they do this when the band broke up?

He rubbed at his aching head, watching the all-girl group The Hippy Chix, deeming them their nearest rivals. One of the duos - The Stevens, a brother and sister double act - were actually quite good. The rest were no competition, confirming Kipper's thoughts. Hmm...

Lost in thought, he jumped when someone knocked on the door. Getting up to answer it, he wondered if he would ever settle down; tired of being on edge all the time. It was one of his students, dropping off an assignment and apologising for missing that morning's class, giving a fairly feasible excuse.

Jason shut the door again, leaning back against it, wondering how the Final would be judged. There was only one person in Impervious who could tell him...

"Initially, it's a knockout. Only the best four will stay on." Hamish watched him across the desk: Jason nodded. "We had to think of something for the benefit of the TV, so there will be a public vote to determine the overall winner." Hamish smiled at him.

Jason nodded again, suddenly feeling tired.

"When did you say you were to have the stitches removed?"

"Thursday afternoon. I have no classes, so I thought that was best. I've caused enough disruption already."

"Come now," Hamish was giving him a sympathetic look, "it wasn't your fault." He sighed. "If we'd had a better security system installed, it wouldn't have happened in the first place."

Jason shrugged. "If they were that determined, they would've found a way in regardless."

Hamish smiled his thanks, knowing what had been said was true, but even so...

"Did you postpone the Final for me?" Jason laughed as he said it aloud. "I know that sounds ludicrous, but it seemed too much of a coincidence. Or was it TV scheduling?"

Hamish's smile broadened. "Right second time."

"I think too highly of myself sometimes, sorry." Jason shook his head, unable to believe he'd come out with that. And in front of Hamish too!

"You are right to. You have quite a talent." He paused. "I decided to postpone for several reasons." He winked at Jason.

A slow smile spread over Jason's face. "Thanks."

"Remember our first conversation, Jason."

Jason cast his mind back, recalling Hamish had been voting for him all the time. His smile spread further.

Chapter 27

The groups had decided Thursday would be their free night this week, letting Jason rest after his procedure. He'd been adamant it would be fine and they didn't have to make allowances for him, but they'd won in the end.

In all honesty, he was relieved to head back to his flat and have some quiet time to let his pounding head settle down. Georgie was coming over at eight, and he'd promised to meet her at the station, on the north entrance, determined not to miss her this time.

He fell onto the sofa, falling asleep for a few hours until his neighbour in the downstairs flat banged his door violently, snapping Jason from his dreamless sleep. His eye fell on the time and he leapt to his feet. 6.50 pm.

He swore. There was so much to do before he had to leave... He dashed to the kitchen, slipping the wine bottle into the fridge, careful in his selection to chose Georgie's favourite. Thankful for microwaveable express rice, he returned to the fridge, taking chicken and vegetables out, chopping them up and sliding them into the awaiting casserole dish, adding a stock cube and boiling water, giving the concoction a stir before wrestling it into the tiny oven and closing the door. Next was the bathroom.

Twenty minutes later, he emerged, a fluffy white towel around his waist, his face still stinging from the rather quick shave. His hair wasn't as well trimmed as normal, and the extra length mostly kept the angry red scar across his forehead hidden. A glance in the mirror showed his complexion was no longer sallow, still pale but healthier; no doubt something Christopher would comment on.

Jason groaned: Christopher. He was meant to phone him when he returned from the hospital! Quickly he stepped into his clothes, grabbing the phone and dialling his brother's number as he sat on the edge of the bed, lacing up his shoes.

"Going somewhere?" Christopher teased him.

"Yes." Jason decided to tease back, seeing as Christopher was in a good mood. "Sorry if that comes as a surprise to you."

Christopher laughed. "Anyone I know?" He saw Jason's face fall and laughed harder. "How's her new job?"

"She hasn't told me much really. That's what tonight is about."

"Oh yes?" Christopher raised one eyebrow inquisitively and they both laughed. "Where are you going? I don't want to end up in the same restaurant."

"You're going out?" Surprise sounded in Jason's voice.

"I'm allowed a life too!" Christopher teased.

"Of course you are! It's just..." He shrugged. "Anyone I know?" He repeated with a smile.

Christopher grinned at him. "Yes - your friend from the train."

"Sabrina?" Jason stopped in mid-tie.

There was a pause as the brothers read each other's expressions. "There's nothing going on between the two of you, is there?" Christopher quizzed.

"No." Jason couldn't stop the flushing of his cheeks. "But... well, she's not exactly your type."

"How would you know?" Christopher laughed, waggling his finger mockingly at Jason. "You can't have both of them."

"Hey, I don't want both of them!" Jason took offence to this. "She told me she had a boyfriend."

Christopher shrugged. "He's history."

"Well, have a nice time."

"I intend to." Christopher winked at him. "I've asked her to model her latest range for me."

It took Jason a second to realise what he was talking about... Sabrina's underwear collection.

"You dirty..."

Christopher just laughed as they hung up. Jason shook his head, picking up his wristwatch from the dresser: 7.45 pm. He mulled over their conversation as he made his final preparations.

Why was he so shocked? He'd left Sabrina with Christopher at Fats, he remembered now, and when he had looked across later that night they seemed to be getting on well.

Was that a twinge of jealousy in his gut? But he had Georgie. Georgie was wonderful; perfect for him, if not too perfect. He didn't quite believe his good fortune that she wanted *him*. He couldn't live without her, if he was honest with himself. It had been - almost - worth the pain just to have her near; he revelled in her touch and the sense of calm and comfort she brought him. That was what love was about. Wasn't it?

WHEN THE SAX MAN PLAYS PART 1 MAKING IT

In the last two weeks, he'd learnt so much. His number one's were Christopher and Georgie, he realised and that was why he was looking forward to getting closer to her.

He sighed, closing the door behind him, ensuring it was locked before he took the steps down to street level. He vowed to be as supportive of her as she had been with him. Theirs would be a strong, loving and tender relationship. He just hoped his lack of experience wouldn't stand in the way. His mind flicked back to his brother - how could Christopher be so brazen, to be admiring his date's underwear on their first time together!

He shook his head, lost in his thoughts, subconsciously watching the streams of commuters heading home, trying to spot her in the masses. Suddenly their eyes met and they smiled the same smile.

"I'm never going to find my own place!" Frustration torn at Georgie, dreading being stuck at home with her parents for another few months, never mind years.

Anna took another mouthful of her drink, glad on this occasion it was just the two of them. "Where's this come from? A year ago you were happy to stay."

"Yeah, well, a lot happens in a year." She sighed. "I want my own space. I don't want my parents running my life forever."

"That's an exaggeration, surely." Anna gave her a serious look. Georgie shook her head, pulling a face.

Anna changed the subject. "What do they think about Jason?"

"They want to meet him." Georgie looked fearfully at her.

"That's okay." Anna laughed. "They won't eat him!"

"They might." Georgie said under her breath.

Anna laughed louder. "What does Jason think about this?"

"I haven't told him yet." Georgie let her breath out slowly. "I'm afraid it'll scare him off."

"Your parents aren't that bad." Anna shook her head.

"But..." She sighed again, taking a gulp of her drink, wishing it was alcoholic. "My father will do the heavy-handed stuff."

"Like?"

Georgie's gaze dropped to the table. "Like you will marry my daughter if you get her pregnant."

Anna's head filled with questions: she pondered which ones to voice. "But you're not having sex, yet. And he wants to marry you anyway, isn't that what Christopher said?"

Georgie nodded again.

"So there's no problem." Anna took a deep breath. "Lay your cards on the table. If you take them into your confidence, it'll save all the embarrassment."

Georgie knew what she was saying made sense; she nodded.

"Maybe it'll be easier if you let your mum do it." She saw Georgie look up, her expression astounded. "Woman to woman would be easier, and let her tell your father what the state of play is." Anna let this sink in, seeing Georgie nod again after a few minutes. "Okay?"

Georgie nodded, realising it was time to 'meet the boys'. She   .

hugged her friend and made her way towards the Music block.

It seemed like years since they'd first heard Jason's solo saxophone music drifting over to him. They had all admired him - talented and good looking, with that distinguished flame-red hair, smattering of freckles and vibrant green eyes. Never had she thought that she would be with him six months down the line...

Last night's conversation still rolled around her mind. Jason was very sweet. He always made sensible suggestions to her dilemmas: he'd told her that it would all work out, telling her not to worry. But Georgie couldn't see it...

Jason was pleased both groups were performing well, despite his recent absence. He'd been surprised to hear that they'd continued to practice without him; this of all things proved that they were in it to win!

Until the Final, they concentrated on the second song, which was coming along nicely. Everyone performed exceptionally well, so much so that Jason privately thought the difference between the two bands was minimal.

As for Georgie; he wasn't sure how they would treat their relationship when they were in the company of others, but they were sticking to working on a professional level for now. He smiled to himself, unsure what they would do if Georgie's Guys were to win - how would they restrain themselves when the excitement was fizzing through their blood?

Last night had been quite a turning point for them both, laying down ground rules and opening their hearts and minds. They both wanted the same thing - a serious relationship. He told her he would respect her decision to take things slowly between them, telling her the universal truth - that the best relationships were founded on friendship.

This had put Georgie at ease - it was sublimely easy to be herself in his presence. They shared ideas for indulging each other's whims - champagne picnics; city river tours at twilight; concert tickets for their favourite artists; theatre visits to see musicals and plays; quiet nights with candlelit dinners and a selection of good music and superb wine; an occasional weekend away. Jason's grin had widened as the night went on, relieved that when his heart had chosen to fall in love with her, it had chosen well.

Georgie, secretly, worried that they would be too friendly and that would make forging a proper relationship difficult. It was nearly overwhelming that he respected her wishes, agreeing when she admitted she wanted commitment before she took the plunge. Her words mirrored Jason's own feelings, which was why it was so easy for him to agree.

The time soon past: soon he was ushering them out, pulling up his collar against the chill in the evening air. They walked as a group to the Underground, getting on the same train, agreeing to meet up again the following Monday. A time that seemed so far away, yet so near... Jason sighed wistfully.

"What was that sigh for?" Georgie leant her head against his shoulder, looking up at him.

Jason laughed to himself. "I guess it's just an end-of-the-week sigh. You know."

"Yeah." She too sighed, and they both laughed.

His gaze locked with hers, reading her expression. "What're you thinking about?"

"I want to come home with you." She sighed. "But I said I'd go home."

"Phone your parents, tell them you've changed your mind."

She shook her head. "They won't like it." She took a deep breath, plunging in. "They want you to come round for Sunday lunch." She gave a little shudder.

"A Sunday grilling?" Jason prompted, seeing her smile. "Make sure I'm worthy enough to be your suitor?"

"Something like that."

Jason nodded. "What time do you need me there?"

Georgie's eyes widened.

Jason laughed, taking her nearest hand. "You said this would happen, sooner or later. I'll be the perfect gentleman, I promise." He hugged her, kissing her head as he knew she liked.

"You couldn't be anything else." She said softly, squeezing him, dialling in the familiar number.

An hour later, she was perched on his sofa beside him, watching as he poured their tea. "How can we go from friends to lovers?"

"Plenty people do. You can be in a loving relationship without sex - sex isn't the be-all and end-all."

Georgie laughed. "It helps."

"Don't get me wrong, Georgie. I'm ready to make love to you right now." He was glad to raise a smile from her. "But that's not what you want." He paused. "Is it?"

"I don't know." She sighed. "I'm so unsure, about everything." To her disgust, she realised she was on the verge of tears.

"In that case, I'm glad you're staying with me tonight." He hugged her in tightly, wondering if this was the right time, nonetheless plunging in. "I have a way around your living problem. You stay here, with me."

"Here?" Georgie's eyes grew saucer-wide, and she pulled away from him, getting to her feet.

"Why not? It's safe; you can live rent-free; good transport links; as much time in the bathroom as you want; even breakfast in bed if you wish." He ticked the plus-points off on his fingers. She laughed at his list, realising he was serious. "There's no hurry to decide. You're welcome anytime." He saw her expression soften, and thought *what the hell...* "To be honest, I love the idea."

"You do?" She gasped, sitting down again.

Jason was nodding ecstatically. "The thought of having you here waiting for me would make the day so much better." He leant towards her, whispering in her ear. "Seriously. The idea drives me wild."

His breath on her skin sent a little tingle through her. "You're serious?" She croaked, feeling the excitement expanding in her stomach.

He nodded, watching the beam spreading across her face. "I'll get us something stronger to celebrate."

She nodded and he got up, walking through to the kitchen, the swing door closing behind him.

"If only you knew how much." He whispered to himself.

Chapter 28

Nervously, he ran a finger around his collar as he waited on the doorstep, waiting to be let in. He hadn't seen Georgie since the previous day; 24 hours that seemed unnecessarily long.

Realising he was clutching at the neck of the wine bottle he'd brought, he laughed at himself, trying to relax. Georgie had built her parents up as complete ogres, but he shouldn't allow this to cloud his judgement.

He was immensely relieved when Georgie herself opened the door, she could see it in his face. It was so strange to see him in their house; the house where nobody felt welcome. Georgie tried to suppress a shudder as she lead him through to the lounge, where her parents were waiting.

Having been introduced, he offered his host the wine. Georgie's father, Herbert, frowned, telling him they did not drink; and that alcohol was the curse of the devil. Jason did not know where to look. He was thankful at least that the rose bouquet had gone down well with Josephine, Georgie's mother. She had thanked him and used the excuse to retrieve a vase from the kitchen, taking also the pro-offered bottle from Jason, throwing her daughter a small, tight smile before she disappeared. Herbert followed, shutting the door behind them.

Padding across the room to eavesdrop behind the closed door, Georgie strained to hear their secret discussion.

"He's a nice fellow." She heard her mother say.

WHEN THE SAX MAN PLAYS PART 1 MAKING IT

"Alcohol!" Georgie could imagine her father shaking his head. "Imagine!"

"He was only being polite, Herb. It was a nice gesture."

Georgie heard her father snort, and bang some pans around, as he did when he was out of his comfort zone. Whether this was because of Jason's presence, or how his wife had taken to their guest, she didn't know. Quickly, she retreated to the sofa, whispering to him that he'd made the right first impression. Jason laughed, just as Josephine re-emerged, thanking him again for the roses and offering him a drink. Jason paused.

"We can open your wine, if you like." She offered.

Jason took it as a white flag, and hesitated. Did he say yes, and give the impression that he'd only brought the wine so that he could consume it himself? Or did he refuse, politely?

"Thank you, water will be fine."

Minutes later, Josephine returned with two glasses of flat mineral water, which she placed on identical mats on the sparkling glass coffee table. Everything was immaculate in the house. Even in his polished shoes, new suit and co-ordinated tie, Jason felt shabby. He'd called into the barbers earlier to have a trim specially for this occasion, exposing the scarring on his forehead. He realised then Josephine was smiling at him, and that alone relaxed both Jason and Georgie. *One down, one to go...*

Jason only let his breath out hours later when he was safely at home. Georgie had stayed with her parents, kissing him goodbye on the doorstep, promising to call him later. He poured himself a large glass of wine, taking a huge gulp before sinking into the sofa, just as his phone bleeped a message.

DON'T WORRY ABOUT FATHER, HE DOESN'T LIKE ANYONE. MUM SAYS YOU'RE WELCOME ANYTIME. I'D SAY YOU PASSED! CU 2MRW. G XXX

The smile crept over his lips, feeling further restored by another gulp of wine. Only then, he found the strength to reply.

FEEL COMPLETELY DRAINED! THANX 4 VOTE OF CONFIDENCE! SEE YOU 2MRW. LUVM. J XXX

It took Georgie a minute to work out what the initials meant... and the smile stayed with her for the rest of the evening.

One problem niggled Jason regarding his second song choice for Georgie's Guys. The song was by American, Carlene Carter. Georgie clearly was not American; neither had she heard of the two Country artists referred to in the song. Nonetheless, she convinced him that the song worked.

In fact, she loved it so much she knew it would win them votes, and wished it had been her first choice! It was clever and funny, with a catchy tune - even the rest of the group were singing along by Monday evening. This had Jason doubled up laughing. Would life in the studio be like this if they won the recording contract?

WHEN THE SAX MAN PLAYS PART 1 MAKING IT

He put the idea to Georgie that she should perhaps have a change of outfit for the second song, suggesting cowboy boots, plaid shirt and a denim skirt.

"You'll be wanting me to wear a Stetson next!" She laughed, agreeing it was a good idea, hoping it would help the audience get into the song.

"What do you want me to wear?" Michael chipped in when the laughter died down.

"What would you feel more comfortable in?" Jason threw the question right back at him.

"I...I don't know. I hadn't thought about it."

Vince frowned. "What's wrong with what you've been wearing?" He saw the rest of the group look at him. "Or am I missing the point? Should we all get specially dressed up?"

"It might be an idea to make an effort," Jason pondered aloud.

Kipper moaned. "Don't make me go shopping with you lot!"

"Hey, there's nothing wrong with us!" Dave snapped back. "It's you who takes three hours in the changing rooms!"

The rest of the group laughed, while Dave frowned. "I wish it was funny! I walked off last time."

"And I wondered where the hell you were!" Kipper too laughed, able to see the funny side, despite the fact that he was the butt of the joke.

Mentally, Jason took a step back. Was it his imagination or had Kipper discovered a self-depreciating sense of humour?

A change had come over the group since they were formed.

His eye landed on Vince - the only one yet to approach him with the answer to his own personal dilemma.

"It's time to go." Georgie saw it was gone eight-thirty and knew her friends were waiting for them.

This had become a Monday evening ritual, and one everyone enjoyed. Jason watched as Kipper fell into conversation with Leanne; Dave sat beside Sophie and Vince beamed at Anna. His face displayed his thoughts: *what was going on?*

"They've become groupies." Georgie whispered in his ear. His flabbergasted expression sent her into fits of giggles. "It keeps them off our back." She confessed, dragging him up to the bar to order a round of drinks.

They leant against the bar as Smithy fulfilled their order.

"You weren't too..." She paused, searching for the right word, "...shell-shocked last night, were you?"

Jason shook his head. "I'm sure your father's a pussycat when you get to know him, and your mother is really sweet." He sighed. "I wish I could say the same about mine."

"I couldn't believe it when she told me." Georgie too shook her head. "The girls get a grudging return invite, but yours was issued without pain." She laughed a little. "My father will soften towards you, in time."

"He'll have to." Jason swallowed a mouthful of his drink. "I'm not going anywhere." He looked at her. "So how did it go when you dropped your bombshell about moving out?"

Her gaze dropped to the floor. "I haven't told them yet."

"It doesn't matter; there's plenty time." Jason shrugged. After all, they'd only discussed the idea, no dates had been mentioned. "I can understand why you want out of there. I'm surprised they didn't sterilise me as I came in the door!"

"They were quite taken with you." Georgie admitted, smiling at him. "Quite a feat."

He raised his glass to her. "Thank you." He leant over to kiss her, interrupted by a loud jeer from the table of thirsty drinkers. As he turned to collect the drinks tray, Smithy winked at him.

Jason laughed at Hamish's request that they do an introduction each for the TV programme. When he relayed this information to the band members, everyone's reaction was different. Kipper proclaimed it was 'right up his street'; Michael and Georgie just looked at each other; Vince raised an eyebrow and Dave looked horrified, despite his new found confidence.

Most of the Tuesday evening was spent coming up with ideas for how they would all be portrayed. Being the photographer, Vince should be filmed on location, according to Kipper. Georgie should be in the library, as she was leaving for the big wide world. Dave could be in the classroom with his French essays, and he and Michael would be filmed in their classes, interacting with their fellow students. Jason would, of course, be filmed during lectures.

Decisions made, Jason called a halt, having arranged to meet Christopher later that night for their usual monthly catch-up.

Christopher's eyebrows had raised when they'd made this plan, especially as not long ago they'd enjoyed this 'monthly meeting'.

During their meal, Jason told him of the developments in his relationship with Georgie. Christopher topped up his wine glass as he spoke. He thought the meal with the in-laws was hilarious, and a positive sign, agreeing with Jason that Georgie's father would need time to get used to the fact that his daughter had a life of her own. He warned him to advance slowly.

Conversation switched to his relationship with Sabrina. This time Jason felt no stab of jealousy as Christopher portrayed their time together as wonderfully relaxing and intimate. He wished only for this sort of evening for himself and Georgie, knowing he just had to be patient.

Days later, in their usual seat in the Union Bar, Jason tapped his keys against his wine glass, catching everyone's attention. "In two days, guys, it'll all be over. The contest winners will be in a completely different world." He paused, while they all took this in. "I want to thank you all for having faith in me, and making my job a hell of a lot easier." He cleared his throat. "You all know what I was up against. You all were my key to unlock this existence. I can't believe all this will be over soon." He shook his head. "I never thought I'd be tutoring two finalists!" He raised his glass, and the group did the same. "May the best group win!"

WHEN THE SAX MAN PLAYS PART 1 MAKING IT
Chapter 29

<u>Impervious College's Annual Talent Competition Finale</u>

The difference was remarkable. Gone were the jests between the groups; the air was thick with tension. Last night, they'd had a rehearsal onstage, filmed as extra material for the programme.

They had drawn lots and Georgie's Guys found themselves playing last; by then, most of their competitors had left. Jason was surprised to see that The Stevens and The Hippy Chix remained. It was almost as if they knew something the others didn't...

The trouble started when Kipper suggested they run through both songs. Both? Jason could see them mutter, but they shrugged their agreement; horrified as Jason's place behind the drums was taken by Vince as Jason picked up his saxophone. When both of Jason's groups performed a second song, they knew they were one step behind: discussions became heated as Jason was accused of 'fixing', and the rest of the band jumped to his defence.

Jason shook his head, clearing his thoughts as their names were announced in playing order. Georgie's Guys were called first, and for the first time in the whole competition, Miracle followed. He winced: talk about heaping on the pressure! He saw even Dave's new positive demeanour sink. "Don't worry, there's always a minute break between songs, it'll be fine." He soothed when they began to protest. "We cannot allow ourselves to think we're better than everyone else and need to be treated as such." He warned, seeing the look cross Kipper's face, taking them backstage to prepare.

Jason couldn't help but notice how much whispering in Dave's ear Georgie did. Kipper and Vince were psyching Michael up for "the performance of his life" as Kipper enthused. Right then, Jason realised that he'd been replaced. *He* did that. *He* was the constant reassurer. He sighed, turning away from the group; at that same moment, Hamish announced the start of the Final.

Jason took a deep breath, smiling at the group before leading them across the stage, feeling the excited tension radiating from them all. Onstage, it was difficult not to get swept away. He sat down, adjusting the stool at the drum kit, surveying the equipment as he usual. Whoever was behind the nuisance - Kipper's attacker; the vandals; his two attackers - Jason felt sure they weren't finished yet. Everything looked perfect and ready to go. He gave them the nod, counting them in.

The microphone in Georgie's hand gave an almighty crackle of static feedback, the ear-splitting noise silencing the crowd. It was dead. Instantly, Jason gave Michael a nod, who was waiting in the wings, and he brought on the high-tech microphone requiring no wiring, a present Jason had given him earlier. He passed it to Georgie, and their song began.

The roar of applause rang in their ears as they bowed, waved and waited for the initial grading. This was a new part to the competition. Each audience member had a range of cards - high, medium and low. The majority showed a rating of 'high' and Georgie's Guys exited the stage, feeling confident.

"How did you know?" Georgie turned to Jason, who was examining his drumsticks and frowning.

He shook his head and strode off, returning with Hamish, both of them examining microphones, lecterns, instruments and lights. Three of the four microphones had been sabotaged; guitar strings had been cut; and the amp wiring had been spliced. Jason shook his head, kicking himself for not seeing this coming.

Gathering together, he lead them to down the Music section, unlocking the supply cupboard (which was more like a third room) and passing around instruments. Admittedly, they were a little worse for wear from the rough usage of former students, but they were better than no instruments at all. Vince and Kipper carried two amps each back to the stage; Jason had two electric guitars in his grip; Michael a box full of new microphones.

Without further delay, he led Miracle onstage to perform, dread churning his stomach when he picked up his saxophone. They wouldn't dare, would they? Everyone in the room had the same thought, at the same time. Jason felt physically sick, and for a moment didn't want to try it: the instrument was much more to him than just a tool of the craft.

He realised then everyone was looking at him; they were wearing the same fearful look that was etched into his face. The vandals hadn't punctured the drums, and that was a novelty, for they were the easiest instrument to ruin.

"Please test the instrument so we can continue." A voice from the judging panel sailed across the stage.

Jason nodded numbly, holding his breath as he cradled the body of his saxophone closer. Breathing out slowly, he closed his eyes as he blew into the mouthpiece, his fingers working automatically through every note. Riotous clapping and cheering broke out as it became obvious that all was well. The five onstage grinned and burst into song while the audience was still going wild.

Another pause while the audience voted - the result a mixture of 'high' and 'medium'. Dave caught Jason's eye and nodded: Jason hid his smile. It all depended on the voting for who the two with instant byes into the final round were. Georgie's Guys almost certainly had won one of those two places, but Miracle seemingly had to fight it out. They watched and waited as the other six performers collected their votes. The last three hadn't achieved a high enough score to be in the final round, and were instantly eliminated.

Jason nodded to himself as The Hippy Chix collected a mixed 'high' and 'medium' vote; as did The Stevens, and the surprise candidates of Rap Skool, the other duo entered.

"CRap more like." Kipper spat, much to everyone's amusement.

This was something nobody had foreseen - four potentials with only three places to fill. Disbelief filled the performers backstage as Hamish announced the judges would now review each performance on the video footage and give each their personal vote, out of ten, starting from the last of the top four - Rap Skool.

Their name sounded even funnier when Hamish said it, and Jason laughed, despite the mounting tension. To be superseded by any of these groups would be unspeakably unjust... He shook his head, wondering if this had been set up for TV? It was just the sort of situation that would add spice to the competition. He sat down beside Michael, who had his head in his hands, unable to watch, already thinking the unthinkable.

Michael's misery was compounded as three of the five judges voted Rap Skool with 9's, the other two votes coming in at 7. Kipper swore, shaking his head solemnly. "I can't believe we could lose to them!"

"Don't say that!" Michael wailed, both Vince's and Georgie's arms around him, as much for his own comfort as theirs.

The Hippy Chix were next, and Jason admired their performance for a second time over the large TV screen. He couldn't believe the scoring when only Hamish raised a 9, the other four lifting 8; 6; 8 and 7. He glanced at the brother and sister duo, who's performance was next to be reviewed, giving them a small smile of encouragement. He was surprised when they walked over to the group.

"They can't vote that trash over us!" Veronica fumed.

Jason was taken aback by her reaction, but couldn't disagree, sharing a sympathetic look with Keith, her brother, who shook his head. "Surely not." He spoke only after their performance had been reviewed.

The judges held their numbers to the crowd - 9; 9; 8; 6; 7.

There was an intake of breath from the crowd as the screen displayed the rankings. Rap Skool - 1st with 41 points; The Stevens - 2nd with 39 points; The Hippy Chix - 3rd with 38 points.

Jason nodded to himself, credit where credit was due, this was a close call! It would make excellent viewing; even the live unruly audience was hypnotised.

Georgie realised then that she didn't want Miracle to lose at this stage. She wasn't sure whether she wanted them to win over her though...

"I can't take this!" Michael jumped to his feet, his eyes wild. "We can't come last, we just can't!" He was on the edge of sobbing, they could all see.

Kipper and Dave were exchanging glances, as they always had done. Vince joined Jason on his feet, linking arms with Michael, trying to calm him as Jason was. Georgie too joined them, unable to watch as Miracle's song played and the crowd inched to the edge of their seats, all eyes on the table in front of the stage, where the judges' number boards displayed 9; 9; 8; 8; 6.

Silence reigned as the room performed the mental calculation. Within seconds, the leader board flashed up the results.

Rap Skool - 41 points; Miracle - 40 points; The Stevens - 39 points; The Hippy Chix - eliminated with 38 points.

WHEN THE SAX MAN PLAYS PART 1 MAKING IT

Michael's scream of relief had Jason again in laughter, leaving the rest of the band shocked but grinning happily, hugging and slapping each other on the back. Thus, the automatic second place was won by Rap Skool, giving them the edge over their competitors, something they took great delight in gloating over.

"Big deal!" Keith hooted, unable to keep the jealousy out of his voice, and huffed away; Veronica chasing after him.

Jason looked at the shell-shocked members of Miracle.

"We can't lose to them, surely?" Kipper swallowed hard, the realisation hitting him suddenly. "They don't even play!"

He was referring to the fact that the two men roared into their microphones over a backing tape.

Jason shrugged. "You get situations like this in contests everywhere." He was aware that everyone was hanging off his words - even Veronica and Keith, who had reappeared from the shadows. "The winner is never the favourite."

"Who's the favourite?" Keith interrupted.

Michael turned around to him. "One of us, of course."

"You cocky git!" Veronica punched his arm. "Why the 'of course'?" She mimicked his voice perfectly and in another situation it might have raised a laugh from the assembled group.

"Think about it." Michael continued, unabashed. "We are the ones with the Music tutor." He gave her a look that implied she was stupid, much to everyone else's hilarity.

Hamish clapped his hands loudly to attract the room's attention. "I want you on in reverse order to play for the title. May the best group win!" He looked at Veronica and Keith. "You're up first, then Miracle, then Rap Skool, then Georgie's Guys. Let's go!"

"Good luck." Jason called as the duo walked onstage with mounting trepidation.

"What the hell are you wishing them luck for?" Kipper spat.

"You have no sportsmanship." Vince shook his head. "I'm surprised you have one brain cell in that big head of yours."

"Be fair." Georgie grinned at him. "He has at least three. One to eat, one to sleep and one to talk."

The group laughed and Kipper realised there was no point reacting to their poking of fun. He cleared his throat. "I'll have you know, I've made the hardest decision of my life recently."

Five heads swivelled to face him. Something in his tone stopped any teasing retorts; instead an interested silence fell.

Jason knew what was coming and was possibly more shocked than the rest. "You have?"

Kipper nodded, a gentle smile lighting his face. "Maya and I are getting a place together. Who knows? A few years down the line we may marry." His smile widened at their collective shock and amazement, the silence only broken by the rippling applause signifying that The Stevens had finished their song, heralding much activity backstage.

The judges gave the pair: 9 (Hamish again!); 8; 7; 7; 6. It was the same judge consistently showing the number 6, and the audience booed.

"We should do something different." Michael said, tugging

frantically at Jason's sleeve. "What can we do?"

Jason shook his head. "Don't tamper with what you've got."

"But we won't win!" Michael had whipped himself into a frenzy.

"Only the best will win." Georgie reminded him.

"Oh yes." Michael spun on his heel, sarcasm dripping from his voice. "You would know all about that, wouldn't you?"

Georgie's hands were on her hips. "What does that mean?"

"You're only here to win Jason's heart." He stated.

"What?!" Jason, Dave and Vince said together.

"It's true." Kipper smirked.

Georgie stood open-mouthed as they departed onstage without her. Jason looked truly hurt, and that pained her the most. But it *was* true. In the beginning, that was the aim - to become close to him. But it was so much more than that now.

She had the man, yes, but she wanted the glory also. She was looking forward to winning the recording contract, even if it was a one-off. She was sure her life was going in the wrong direction and she was determined to fight the tide to correct her path. Was being the operative word, she realised in horror. The edges of the dream were crumbling...

"I don't believe you don't care." Dave was the first one towards her, a note of sadness creeping into his voice.

Georgie realised she'd missed the voting and kicked herself, knowing that this proved she wasn't interested anymore, which was far from the truth. She looked at the group. Michael was beaming ecstatically, as were Vince and Jason - who wouldn't catch her eye.

"Three nines!" Michael gurgled gleefully. "We can't lose with three nines!"

"This means more to me than I thought it ever would." She admitted, looking at him as he sat down beside her.

"Tell them that." Dave nodded at the group, giving her a gentle nudge off the ledge they were perched on.

The group shared a grin as the votes for Rap Skool were announced: 6 (from Hamish, which confused Jason as he'd been voting everyone 9's all night); 7; 7; 8; 6.

"Before we begin," Georgie strode onto the stage in front of Jason, Kipper and Dave, addressing the audience. "I want to take this opportunity to say a few words of thanks. Firstly to Impervious, for holding the event." She paused for the polite clapping that followed. "To Hamish for arranging the publicity and the prize!" She paused again as the applause increased. "And to my fellow performers. I want to thank them for their dedication and hard work; and most importantly, for their faith in me. I never dreamed we'd get this far and I know they agree with me when I say that we couldn't have done it without Impervious' Music tutor, Jason Bottelli."

Jason's expression froze as the spotlight found him, blushing as the audience rose to their feet, cheering and applauding. He began to beat out the intro to the song and the others scurried into position, all grinning at each other. Miracle had achieved the highest score so far of 42 with those three 9's, an 8 and a 7. It was a tall order to beat their high score but Georgie gave it her all, holding her breath as the judges raised their number boards.

Hamish raised his 9, blowing Georgie a kiss as he did so. Then followed an 8, another 9, and another 8. The fifth judge was the man who'd been voting 6's. Georgie bit her lip, her arms around Dave and Kipper as they waited.

Another 8 would tie the two groups, Jason caught himself thinking, *but was that allowed?*

Another 8 was raised to equal boos and cheers from the crowd, but Hamish leapt to his feet like a true professional. "We have a tie-break situation, folks!" He beamed. "With a kick!" He showed the video that had been taken during the previous evening's rehearsal. "I understand both groups were so sure they would win, they concocted a second song to perform for us! I say they play that second song and we decide on the merits of both performances!"

Chapter 30

The crowd were at first horrified, and then they loved the idea, chants going up for the second performance! Jason looked at the group, shocked. *A stand off between the two!*

"Let the boy go first!" Hamish indicated Michael to the crowd and a huge cheer arose. Jason just smiled.

"Can he do that?" Kipper hissed.

"It says in the small print, he can." Vince grinned.

"What small print?" Kipper frowned.

"In the programme." Vince waved his hand towards the big screen, which was displaying clearly the aforementioned small print - which none of the participants had bothered to read. Except Vince, and Jason.

"Oh." It was the only word Kipper could manage.

"I'm glad we're on first, it'll give you time to get into costume." Jason grinned at Georgie, who had the decency to blush. She wished them luck before retiring to find her Country outfit.

"Introduce yourselves." Hamish called across the stage.

Jason nudged Michael forward, who froze until Jason whispered in his ear what to say.

He swallowed hard. "We're Miracle and this is "Englishman in New York". We hope you like it." He gave a shy smile to the crowd and instantly won a few more fans.

Jason began the intro with his saxophone solo, Vince playing softly alongside him, wincing as Dave began a fraction late.

Would anyone notice? Kipper had swapped keyboard for piano and it sounded wonderful. Michael began the lyrics perfectly on cue. Three and a half minutes of stunned silence from the crowd later, Jason finished with twenty seconds of saxophone solo, which nearly brought the roof down!

The five stood, breathless with excitement and nerves, awaiting the judges' responses. Hamish gave the thumbs up, something which always made Jason laugh. Their praise reverted around his ears.

"Superb team effort!"

"An improvement on the original entry."

"A fun rendition of a popular song."

"A jazzy, catchy tune which gets your feet tapping."

Jason ushered the group offstage while the audience screamed their names. As he set eyes on Georgie, his heartbeat doubled. She wore a blue and red check shirt, denim skirt and black leather cowboy boots with a matching black Stetson. She had several, in fact, which she handed out to Dave, Vince, Kipper and Jason, who all looked at her questioningly and laughed.

Knowing that Michael would feel left out, she placed one with a pink feather on it on his head as she walked past, much to his delight and everyone's amusement.

Onstage, she launched straight into their introduction. "We're Georgie's Guys. This is a number by American Country artist, Carlene Carter. I'm sure you'll like it as much as we do. It's called "I Feel Lucky!" and yes before anyone asks, I do." She gave the crowd her best grin, beckoning the men onstage, laughing as they jokingly pulled oh-not-again! faces.

Precious seconds in, Kipper was tinkling the ivories, Jason and Dave were playing in complete harmony and Vince was completely at home on the drums. Georgie launched into the song, swaying her hips and nodding her head with the music. She had to admit Kipper played rather professionally: he had several piano solos that sounded just like the original recording. The song finished with Vince and Kipper, and they could have sworn the cheers were louder this time around.

The judging panel were as enthusiastic as ever, with Hamish leading the way. "My girl, you have a great voice. With your talented friends, you could go far!" He gave them a grin and another thumbs up.

Again Jason laughed, part of him wondering if he was going to wake up sometime soon...

"Great piece, beautifully presented!"

"Loved the way that everything tied together, well done!"

"Wonderful song!"

"A perfect performance from a talented group."

Jason beckoned Michael onstage, and the crowd laughed at his fetching cowboy hat complete with pink feather. He stood with Georgie in the middle of the stage, flanked on the right by Kipper and Dave, with Vince and Jason on their left.

"Can we run the tape again?" Hamish asked.

The crowd mock-groaned, and the two groups turned to the

screen to watch their own performances. Then Hamish sent them backstage while the judges discussed the performances.

While the rest were deep in conversation, Jason led Georgie to a quiet corner of the room. Intrigued, she let herself be guided, her mind still buzzing with the thrill of performing and the thought that they could win... She barely heard what he whispered in her ear, and what she heard, she felt sure she'd imagined. Looking around them, she saw they had stolen all the attention, and when she turned back, Jason was on one knee.

She allowed him to take her left hand, covering her mouth with her free right hand, unable to believe her eyes - knowing what was coming.

"I know we haven't been together long, and I know things haven't exactly run smoothly, but what happened convinced me that you're the only one for me, Georgie. I never want to be without you, I love you. Will you marry me?"

There was a stunned silence in the room.

Jason had locked eyes with her, watching tears fill her eyes. His heart hammered as he fumbled for the ring box in his pocket, revealing with shaking hands the ring he'd chosen only yesterday - a platinum diamond ring.

Ecstatic joy filled her expression. "I...I don't know what to say."

"How about a 'yes'?" Kipper joked, but his voice was full of shock and happiness.

The room laughed, including Jason and Georgie.

"It seems such a humble word, but yes I will marry you." She let him guide the ring onto her finger, still with shaky hands; then they embraced, and the room burst into applause. Seconds later they were called back to face the decision.

"Before anything else happens," Kipper grinned as he strode onstage, "there's something you all should know. Jason just asked his girlfriend if she'd marry him - and she said yes!"

For the benefit of the TV viewers, there was a close-up of Georgie's left hand as the pair strode across the stage, both grinning.

A loud cheer arose from the audience, making both of them blush, before Hamish called for silence. He announced that the decider would be made by the nation. There were only thirty minutes to vote, he gave details of the two phone numbers: the one ending in -01 for Miracle, the -02 for Georgie's Guys.

Jason knew the cameras were following them as they yet again headed backstage. The group were grinning at him, and he too felt their excitement. They were on the cusp of what could be the start of something truly special; something life-changing.

"Will they vote for both of us?" Georgie's question broke his thoughts.

Jason laughed aloud.

"You know what I mean." Playfully she slapped his arm. "What if the nation votes equally?"

"Then we have to share the recording contract, right?" Vince looked to him for confirmation.

Jason nodded.

"Is that allowed?" Michael was hurt by this suggestion.

Jason shrugged, aware that they were looking to him for all the answers; answers he just didn't have.

"Who do you think will win?" Kipper came straight out with the question. "You're the music man, you should know!"

"I don't know how millions of people are going to vote!" Jason laughed, aware Kipper had indeed hit upon the truth.

"But what do you think?" Kipper pressed, seeing Jason grow uncomfortable under the weight of the question.

"It's a close call," he admitted.

"But?" Kipper prompted.

"Leave him alone." Dave cut in. "It doesn't matter what anyone thinks, it's what the nation wants."

"What do you know?" Kipper turned on his friend.

Dave shrugged. "This is the fairest way to achieve a winner."

"A bloody cop-out you mean." Kipper huffed.

"I think it's great." Vince began. "You've got the best elements for TV here: a nation's deciding vote, tension and suspense." They all nodded.

"The winners could work with the other group. How great would a collaboration sound?" Vince continued.

Jason found himself nodding, wondering how Vince had managed to read his mind. Of course, that was a perfect solution but they didn't live in a perfect world. It was true that artists *did* have a certain power in the studio, so Vince's suggestion wasn't as bizarre as it first sounded.

He wondered what effect this would have on his life from now on, either way he was on the winning side. He looked at Dave and Kipper, so too were they; technically Vince belonged to the winning side, being his second-in-command. So it was between Georgie and Michael.

The time passed quickly. Soon they were back on the stage, Hamish greeting them as they strode into the lights, the crowd cheering and screaming for their favourite.

"Jason," Hamish rested his arm around Jason's shoulders. "I had no idea when we began this year's competition that you would have such a major influence. You have conquered all, against the odds. Tonight's result will change the lives of all of the performers. I have a feeling your time at Impervious will be short, but I hope it was sweet."

Jason looked at him in horror, his thoughts written across his face. *He was being publicly fired?*

"You said yourself that life for the winners will not be the same, so don't look so surprised!"

The audience laughed.

"And now! The moment we've all been waiting for! The result!" Hamish turned around as the big screen above them was lowered, a series of figures displayed for the audience to see.

"A massive two million viewers around the country voted!" Georgie shuffled towards Jason, taking his nearest hand, unaware that Michael was doing the same on his other side. This action only highlighted the difference between the two groups.

Dave, Kipper and Vince were rooted to the spot, relieved that soon the wait would be over.

Jason cast glances around him: the five he'd tutored and bonded so well with; the audience of Impervious' students and his own companions. Christopher was there with Sabrina, as he expected, and his friends from Fats were also present. He was surprised to see the Club's owner, Glenn, too sat with them, smiling encouragingly at him. He saw Anna, Leanne and Sophie held spellbound, their home-made Georgie's Guys placards frozen in their grip. The image made him smile.

Hamish began, grinning as the stats displayed. "As you can see, there are only a few votes in it." One bar was a fraction higher than the other, one coloured purple, one coloured green. "The final figures came in at 0.99 million and 1.01 million."

"Get on with it!" Kipper murmured, feeling the tension getting to him.

Jason risked a glance at Michael, who had his eyes squeezed tightly shut, unable to watch. Georgie was hypnotised by those bars, urging Hamish to reveal the names under her breath. How could he have doubted her devotion to the contest? She wanted to win with every fibre in her body ...for him. She looked at him, feeling his gaze on her, and they shared a small, nervous smile. He gave both of them a squeeze.

"You can stop now." A voice drifted across the stage, and a man suddenly walked across the stage to shake Hamish's hand. "It doesn't matter who won, I want to work with both groups.

WHEN THE SAX MAN PLAYS PART 1 MAKING IT

They're both winners to me!"

"Ladies and gentlemen, Mr Rae Azeem, our sponsor and the managing director of "Aim Records"!" Hamish beamed, many flashes going off around the room as the two men shook hands.

Concern struck Jason. It was too casual... too friendly; and, damn it, too fake! He let go of Michael and Georgie, walking away, shaking his head. The five remaining onstage looked at each other in bewilderment.

"*I* want to know who won!" Kipper found his voice.

Vince joined in. "I'm sure everyone does." He turned to the audience, who went wild, cheering.

The names flashed up on the board to riotous applause.

Jason heard the auditorium burst into applause, realising they must've made the announcement. He couldn't have cared less who won. The whole thing had been a complete farce, as far as he was concerned, and he felt like a complete idiot for being sucked in.

It wasn't right to mess with their heads in this way; they were not puppets to have their fates decided for them as if the world was only make-believe. Hamish had wanted this result, and he'd pulled many strings to achieve it.

Jason felt physically sick. There was nothing he could do about it. Their fates had been decided. They were in this together, which would have been nice, in a way, if it hadn't left such a bitter taste in his mouth.

WHEN THE SAX MAN PLAYS PART 1 MAKING IT

"What the hell was that about?" Christopher took him by the shoulders, shaking him.

"It's a fix." Jason's voice was flat and lifeless. "The whole bloody thing is a fix!"

"What are you talking about?" Christopher increased his grip, trying to look into his brother's face, seeing Jason's fury rising.

"You wouldn't understand." Jason shook his head, shrugging him off, scenes from the past few months rolling around his mind. Who was in on it? He felt sure Hamish wasn't a sole operator. Soon, the group caught up with him.

"Jas?" Georgie stepped towards him, trying to hug him.

His body stiffened with tension. "Please Georgie, I'm going to explode and I want to do it in peace."

She searched his expression, seeing his crushed, fragile emotions on display. Her kiss received no reply, and as she walked back to the group, Jason disappeared into the black of the night.

He could run miles and miles, let the throbbing pounding of his feet take the stress from him. He could go into the gym; take it out on the punch bags.

But no. Jason was a music man, music was his everything, even now. He'd often searched for solace in his music and this was no different.

Saxophone music filled the night, as it had filled their days, enticing them into this world. The group stood listening, swept away; each rendered speechless.

WHEN THE SAX MAN PLAYS PART 1 MAKING IT